Chaos

Lyudmila Androvska

Published by Lance bv, 2024.

This is a work of fiction. Similarities to real people, places, or events are entirely coincidental.

CHAOS

First edition. October 1, 2024.

Copyright © 2024 Lyudmila Androvska.

ISBN: 978-9080634503

Written by Lyudmila Androvska.

To Valeri

Chaos – disorder, confusion, untidiness, disarray, muddle, misrule, litter, jumble, turmoil, mess, tangle, mix-up, gallimaufry, balderdash, drivel, anarchy, a state of lawlessness, disorganization, derangement, disruption, babel, etc...

1

She was hoping in the black impenetrable murk that the man wouldn't find her. But led by desire and his male instinct, he arrowed into the darkness straight for her and wheezing he squeezed her body. His hand went straight under her skirt, clawed her thighs, ploughing bloody furrows in her skin, scraps of flesh lodged deep under his nails. She knew that resistance was pointless, she went limp, trying not to hear the panting in her ear. For a long time now she'd learnt to separate mind and spirit from what was happening with her body. She even tried to doze a little while the man on top of her exuded a sticky smelly sweat. She half closed her eyes and distanced herself...

And then suddenly something jolted within her. Again the smell wafted over her, the sharp breath of a stallion after a long gallop, homing in on the mare. It came from outside, he was lurking, eavesdropping at the walls of the barn. She felt it, the stink of desire was strong, the man on top of her smelled it too. He sensed how the other man outside was tracking his quivering disquiet. He let out one last gasp, covered her in moist stickiness, got off her, slippery as a slug, and left in a hurry.

She almost saw how the man outside could hardly wait to seize the moment of the first man's disappearance into the distance to rush inside. He fell on her with a wild desire even more enflamed by her exposed wet body and by what had happened while he'd been waiting, and losing no time he immediately slid into her. The panting transferred to her other ear, the smell oppressed her, slimy sperm ran down her thighs, once, twice.

A blue mist penetrated the gaps in the barn and drove the man outside, fearful that his face be exposed. And he sank into the anonymity of the retreating dark, which carried away his features, his name and his slaked thirst.

Coinciding with the dawn, from the same place where the first rays shot out, a small white dot appeared and began to swim towards the shore. It approached slowly; what stood out was the hair, shimmering like a shaft of sunlight, the steady sweep of gentle white arms...By now close to the shore, the young woman stepped on to the bottom, the water barely covering her waist, sprinkling her with pearl drops and melting into the long golden hair. Her steps under the water were invisible, just the white foam of the lapping waves gradually revealed the straight rounded shoulders, the erect breasts, big as a man's hand, the firm compact stomach. The water seethed around her, foamed as if sculpting this slender body, the long thighs, the slim knees, the narrow ankles...

The sea gave birth to a woman, gracious and slight, who'd left her cares and worries behind, had drowned in its deepest waters the dark sludge which had threatened to coat her soul. A Venus with a pale beautiful face, with that indeterminate age which could be seventeen or twenty four. A face with smooth firm skin which showed not only infinite youthfulness, but revealed an ignorance of the world and its matter, which led to credulity and of course problems. A Venus whose name was Petra, and whom they called Homeless.

Every morning even before sunrise Homeless Petra went running to the sea, quickly took off what few clothes she had and threw herself into the cold waves. She swam ever further out, until the shore disappeared from her view, only then did she take a breath of relief, that she'd escaped from land and everything on it. Fatigue and the cold bottomless water gradually soothed the chaos raging in her soul. Petra relaxed on her back and became motionless with eyes closed, all her

CHAOS

senses taking in the infinite and the quiet. Only the lapping of the waves murmured about her and rocked her body.

But the quiet thickened, initially ringing quietly, then becoming louder, until it became a roar, rumbling in her ears, the peace of the abyss began to scare her, her muscles tightened, her body sank in the dark water, which swallowed her slowly in bites. With a few strokes, Petra was swimming again, she looked around and only now she realized how she was alone in infinity, hanging in a space with no support beneath her. Everything scared her – the sea tense in awaiting the sunrise, and the sky lighting up above and below her, and even the first rays, which pierced the surrounding dark. She turned and set off back for the shore. She swam slowly, and rejoiced in the freedom of her body, pure and washed from strangers' touch, experienced every movement, the touch of the water, pinching her wounded thighs and washing away the residue of the night just past.

Homeless Petra lived in the barns of the village. In every one of them there were two or three thick blankets for her, they left food and some other item of clothing. She never decided in advance where she'd spend the night. In the morning she hunted for mussels and whelks in the rocks, and in the afternoon, she entered the forest and gathered herbs for the village women. When fatigue and desire for sleep overtook her, she made for the nearest barn, ate quickly, and tucked herself into the furthest darkest corner. She closed her eyes and before surrendering to sleep, she prayed that no-one would come to her this night. She never slept deeply, she'd doze like a rabbit with ears forever sharpened, and she'd start at every sound.

She felt the steps from afar. Before them, she sensed the smell. The breath of a loner, driven by the wild call of the flesh. Heavy and suffocating the smell got closer with stealthy steps, disguising as far as possible his impatience and lust. Petra rolled into a ball in her distant corner, pressing into the mud wall of the barn, as if to merge into it...

LYUDMILA ANDROVSKA

She didn't remember now whether she was thirteen or fourteen when for the first time at night three men at the same time had held her down, and each taken their turn. She didn't know who they were. Maybe it was that guy who'd met her in the day and given her that undisguised male once-over. The one-time little girl had grown suddenly into a beautiful grown up lassie, a little woman, and he'd wanted her. And like most men, he'd been scared of risking taking her virginity on his own...

From that night on, Petra forgot peaceful sleep. That's why, later, when she married, the first thing she did as a new wife was to sleep, hidden in her husband's house. Protected by a high fence and strong walls of the house, Homeless Petra slept a whole month, waking only to consume hot tasty soups and then sink into oblivious sleep to the horror of her young husband. He fearfully hung around her without knowing what to do and from time to time pressed his ear to her breast, to see if she was breathing.

Every night Petra had visitors, irrespective of what end of the village she found herself in, in which barn she was hiding, or how deeply she was buried in the straw. The men found her everywhere. They waited patiently, knowing that each one would take his turn, even the waiting and the noises from inside enflamed desire even more and gave their imagination free rein.

Some nights it happened that there was just one visit, but that was seldom. Usually there were two or three. And when there was a holiday and during the day in the pub, old man Nacho poured out wine and rakia freely, at night the queue quickly lengthened. But however many the visitors, at the first sign that the sky was lightening, everybody disappeared, Then Petra would pull down her bunched up skirts and crumpled clothes and rush off towards the sea.

That's what she did as well after that first night, when she felt so sullied and she ran towards the sea with sticky thighs, although it was winter.

CHAOS

 Snow rarely stayed in the village, but no-one remembered cold like this ever.

 Petra threw off her clothes and jumped into the sea in the hopes of dying. The cold winter water stopped her breath, cleared her head, and everything seemed so distant and unreal, as though it hadn't happened to her. She swam a long time, until she rid herself of the coating that was stuck to her, and she came out of the icy sea, purified and born anew.

 From that time on, there remained a pain, low down in her stomach, which on cold days cut through her. Later when she found out how children are made, Petra realized that after that swim in the winter sea, she would be left sterile forever. It was better this way, she told herself and felt happy. God had protected her from forever falling pregnant and giving birth to children, where the only thing she'd know was that they were from her. She felt no maternal feeling inside her. It was surely hereditary, hadn't her mother once brought her newly born baby to the door of her father. Or more accurately the guy that she nominated as the father. She'd left her in the night in a little basket, woven from branches and covered in leaves, wrapped in a blanket, and then she'd gone off who knows where. And for years thereafter she'd not called. But Petra never asked about her mother. She felt no daughterly feeling either for the man who looked after her, and who did nothing to gain at least her respect, if not her love. And he'd disappeared from her life long ago without even leaving a roof over her head. And Petra lived out of barns, gathered herbs from the woods, which old Krayanka had pointed out for soups, brought them to the women, in the morning she'd run into the sea even before dawn, afterwards emerging with a refreshed purified soul, put on her clothes – a strange mélange of colours, designs and thicknesses of materials – and slowly made for the village.

2

The village was like an island. From one side the sea bounded it, and on the other three sides it was walled by the forest. The men never went to its other side. They only penetrated as far as where the trees grew thicker, they cut whatever they needed for the boats and their squat houses and returned. Not one of them had ever passed through it, to see what there was beyond, and to tell the others. It was of no interest. Their curiosity extended to their neighbour's house and no further. They accepted that on the other side of the forest there was sea again. That was enough for them...

They lived the life which for centuries their ancestors had lived. The new passed by somewhere to the side of them and did not touch them. They didn't even realize that the world was changing, they stood in frozen passivity, deaf to the calls of transformation. Time had stopped like the pendulum of a broken wall clock. Something had to wind the spring and to swing the pendulum, so as to restart the natural path of development.

They fed off the sea, as their ancestors had, they caught fish and whatever was left over, they sold to the holiday-makers who came by the potholed dusty road. They weighed their fish a long time, as though in two minds, and slyly looked over the newcomers and tried to hold on to them. The holiday-makers would take a turn about the village and who knows why they'd make haste to go back to where they came from, as though something was chasing them. At first they thought that the village had not become a resort because of the high cliff shoreline, with no sand or beaches, but they sensed a particular atmosphere, as though

CHAOS

down a mouse-hole, and they left, not buying what they'd come for. The fishermen weren't angry, the sea was providing less and less fish, often the boats would return empty and in order to feed their children, the women picked salted mackerel from lines strung under the curtains. Mackerel which had dried for years as a reserve for such bad times. The children's lips split because of it, their throats stuck with salt, and their fingers cracked round black bugs, sunk into the dark dry fishy flesh. Now they were unable to feed themselves from the sea, but they didn't leave the land that had given birth to them. They were scared of the infinity that awaited them outside their village, and the unknown which they would encounter there.

The women stopped giving birth, but they got married because that was expected. They expected nothing but they lived in some kind of secret anticipation. They didn't know what it was. It had to be something which would change the steady grey days, would jolt their dead souls with goose bumps, would stir up the frozen air in the village. They'd heard old stories about life with love and death from love. They didn't believe it happened there, in their village, love was something infinitely distant. But maybe that's exactly what they were waiting for. Everyone was waiting for it. The men...And the women...And the old...they'd be the first to understand. Their waiting was close to its end...And the children hoped and lived with quiet patience. They waited with a meek determination, they had a whole life before them.

The shore was rocky, but the boys liked the cliff the best, rising sheer above the sea, on which perched an old deserted house. It had turned grey like the rock and it merged with it from a distance. The children gathered there every day, twenty-thirty metres below them was the roaring crash of the waves, and the children sat and hung their legs over the abyss, staying for hours. They waited patiently. They hoped and dreamed. Here they relived the stories heard in reverie from their grandfathers by the winter fire. And they fixed their eyes there, where the sea and sky merged into a blue line, they saw pirate ships, enormous fish, hurricanes and thunderbolts that split the sea in two. Then the view cleared before their eyes, they looked at the level calm sea, which didn't change and waited for something to emerge. Something lacking, something that still would not appear. Something that would bring a new thrill and scent of adventure into their lives, something that would take them out of the little village and dispatch them into the infinite debris of the world...

The boys sighed, suppressing the obscure chaos, which was forming in their childish souls, and turned their eyes again towards the sea. Their fathers were entering the deep in their fishing boats and after endlessly long hours, they'd set off back to land, so as to set off again the next day again into the deep, and then return to the shore... A circle, which had no beginning or end, which turned them and they took on its inertia, they couldn't escape it, dizzy from its endless revolutions.

The children recognized the boats from afar, they knew which one belonged to whom, checked them one more time, counted them, and disappointed they turned their eyes again outwards to the horizon. And they knew that something would come...

The path that made its way from the cliff to the jetty was steep and stony, hanging over the village. Somewhere in the middle, hidden in the shadow of a walnut tree, Granny Vanda's house jutted out over the sea, as if at any moment it would plunge into it. That tree seemed out of place on that sea coast. Grannie Vanda had planted it many years before, when she was about to give birth to Mavri. She wanted to give birth in the village – she too like the others was scared by the anonymity of the big city – but after two days and nights of labour pains, when the baby's heartbeat became imperceptible and the mother began to turn blue, they placed her in a wagon and set off together with the church sexton. Vanda lacked the strength to protest, but before she was lifted into the wagon, she managed to plant a little round walnut in the crumbly earth in front of the house. Someone had told her that if she planted a walnut, she'd live as long as the tree grew, and its

CHAOS

trunk became as thick as her waist. And this was many, many years ahead...She would survive so many things, in order to look after her son, wait for his father...But she didn't water the walnut for herself, but for the life of her child, which now she did not feel moving inside her. I beg you, Lord, save him for me. Vanda prayed and put her hands over her sagging enormous belly. With her trembling fingers she tried to catch that little quivering sign of life inside her, which she wanted, but for some time did not sense. Save him, Lord God, she prayed, help me bring him up and when his father returns, he'll see that I have looked after his child well...

And while the wagon drove into the distance, Vanda lay in it with her head covered and her eyes fixed on the place where she watered the walnut...

3

Elo turned up in the village from who knows where. Simply one morning they met the dawn with him. And as if along with his arrival, scampering between the houses there were little brown field mice, come from who knows where in these wooded places by the sea.

Elo differed from the dark gloomy fishermen, not only with his bright hair and blue eyes which lit up his anyway pale face. His whole aura was white, bright and pure. There was something intangible, something unpredictable in his behaviour, which slipped under women's surveillance and instinctive judgement, and which fooled them even more. The men also fell for his magnetism, sought his company, stealthily observed him and tried to understand what exactly it was that the women liked so much. It eluded them, it seemed a wonder, but they persisted. They took Elo out fishing, they lined up to invite him to their boats and they sought his close companionship. They copied everything that they saw in him during the day. And in the evening the women hung around the hut, which he'd made at the end of the village, they watched him stringing the fish, helped him fasten it to the neighbouring branches on a breezier spot and looked to catch his eye. Elo smiled, cracked some joke or other, from time to time his eyes sparked, but he didn't allow anything else. Even so the men got irritated and began looking at him with knitted brows.

Elo had grown up in a big city, in a family with an unstable father and continually weeping mother, along with two sisters. One day the father just up and abandoned them. At just eight years old Elo had to play the man of the family. Luckily his big sister took up this role. His

CHAOS

mother, who even before this had the softest spot for him, was now forever seeking him out, monopolising him, hiding him in her arms and washing his face with her tears. Embarrassed and with a cloudy sense of a bad taste in his mouth, Elo disentangled himself, took a breath and in the next moment one of his sisters grabbed him. The eldest sister, an independent girl with a few boyish mannerisms, which subliminally excited him, pulled him to her and quickly ordered him to do something. But in spite of the subjugation she expected from him, he enjoyed her attention. With her he felt as with a friend. And when her grip began to tighten, she was easier to escape than his mother. He'd only just freed himself from his big sister when the other sister reached out for him. She was one year younger than him. Of the three she resembled their father the most, she was slim and delicate, with a mysterious smile and impenetrable gaze. She wound herself round him, meowing like a kitten, stroked him with her soft feathery hands and from this touch and from her scent, his eyes dimmed and his thoughts clouded over. She was the most difficult one to get away from. He often yearned to be left alone, to attend to his troubled soul and try and put it in order, but he never succeeded. When he thought about his mother's tears and her piteous wailing, whenever his father's name was mentioned, Elo preferred to stay under the control of one of his sisters. Usually he sought his big sister, spending time with her was calming and natural, it didn't weigh him down, and the thought that he could always leave and without any difficulties, held him most strongly of all. The presence of the little sister sowed within him additional chaos, it strained his anyway highly strung soul. Some disturbing sense made him to seek her scent with quivering nostrils whenever she was not around.

In this way a number of years flew away, they scattered unheeded beside their silent home. From time to time a little money arrived from their father, barely better than nothing, and forcing their mother to again drown in her tears. His big sister was father and mother in the family and skilfully managed them through life's traps.

Elo continued to experience that agitation in the presence of his little sister. Over the years it had emerged from its previous vagueness, it had formed itself with exact contours into something which shook his body and made his hair stand on end. This frightened him. For a long time he'd realized that his little sister carried within her the same chaos that had given him no peace for years.

Early one morning, when everyone was sleeping, she crept into his room and snuggled trembling into the bed. She lay with her back to him, pressing her little warm bottom into his stomach, and her long straggly blonde hair tickled his nose and wafted that scent of hers which drove him wild. Elo only knew that he could no longer control the chaos within him, it spread through him, enveloping everything and engulfed him.

From that pitch dark the big sister's shout jolted them, she stood by the door with open mouth and even wider open eyes, and neither knew what to do nor was able to do anything.

Elo didn't remember how he'd escaped. He didn't remember what happened before that. The only feeling that he was left with was of the hot lava, which whirled him faster and faster and drove him into the black space of greater chaos...

This memory drove him from place to place and didn't allow him to stop, it made him avoid people and women most of all, he was frightened of the emergence of some smothering love, which would again rivet him to a particular spot.

If the men from the village had realized that his caginess was down to a fear of being branded with a mark of ownership, they would have been a lot more relaxed...

Only when he happened on this village, Elo found that peace in his soul, which he'd always sought. At the beginning he was struck dumb by the torpor, which he perceived in everything here, but later he liked

CHAOS

it and he realized instinctively that his restless soul thirsted for precisely this primitive life, in which nothing happened.

He built himself a hut and lived in it, went with the men to catch fish, learnt how to clean it and soak it in brine and how to hang it on long lines. He was aware of the women's excitement, it pampered and tickled his worldly soul, but he allowed nothing further than distant flirtation and looks. And he didn't want to provoke jealousy and hatred from the men towards him. At night he went to bed in the hut, he dozed, but half awake, he'd hear the quiet stealthy footsteps outside. He knew they were a woman's footsteps, he only had to give a sign and she would enter. Just a tiny sign... But Elo didn't open his eyes and he pretended not to hear anything.

The men realized that their wives and daughters circled him at night. They sucked in their cheeks, knitted their brows and as soon as darkness fell, always two or three took up positions by his hut. Their heavy footsteps scared him. Elo knew that some night they'd just haul him out, their big fists would make a drum out of his body and head, and on the next day his hut would be wrecked. That would be the sign that he had to leave. And then where would he lay his head? With that idea everything rose up inside him, stirred up all his thoughts and a force emerged that he felt would blow up on its own.

One night the men's footsteps weren't heard. It seemed to him that a quiet rustling passed and died down somewhere close to the hut. Elo felt confused, he didn't know if this wasn't the calm before the storm. He didn't close his eyes the whole night, he lay in the dark with eyes wide open, without moving and listened to the tense silence. With the appearance of the first sun's rays, the rustling was heard in the opposite direction and disappeared along with his fears.

The next night the rustling passed again by his hut and died down somewhere close by in the woods. Elo pricked up his ears and kept quiet. He spent the night without sleep, with cloudy muddled thoughts, from which he was pulled by the light sound of rustling in the opposite direction. Elo rushed out of the hut but saw nothing. Only the sun slowly swimming out of the sea…

At night now no-one disturbed him. Elo relaxed in the hut and when he heard the passing of a light breeze, he closed his eyes and was carried away into a carefree sleep. In the morning he'd get up very early, he'd go to the small quay with the boats and watch the men. They pretended not to notice him and as if turned their backs on him, it was as though by chance, but now no-one gave him dirty looks. One by one the cast off into the sea, the quay emptied, only one boat would be rocking on its own at the end. Sometimes in the afternoon Elo would see a young woman around it – the woman would descend from a small house above the sea, untie the boat and launch it with the skill of an old fisherman. She'd take the oars and start rowing. Elo had the hazy feeling that her eyes were fixed on him, but when he turned towards her, her gaze shifted.

Once Elo woke much before dawn, listened out with the intuition that the breeze had not yet passed, and cautiously poked his nose outside.

The young woman was sleeping, sat, lying back on a nearby tree, and on her knees lay a long rifle. Elo came out quickly. The noise made her jump and point the gun barrel at him. Then she saw him, she slowly lowered the gun and the stress shown in her face gradually relaxed into a tender smile.

Vanda and Elo lived in her small house. In the morning he got up like everyone else and went to the quay. The men began again to gather round him, they offered advice, helped him launch the boat into the water and to string the lures.

Elo was one of them.

4

Vanda was in love. She adored this man who'd appeared in the village from no-one knew where, won the women's hearts and the hatred of the men. And perhaps stressed by this hatred and the obscure threats which drifted in the surrounding air, he married her unexpectedly quickly and the pair of them hid themselves in the cottage above the sea. Vanda wasn't concerned about why he'd taken this sudden decision. She'd won the unspoken gratitude of the men and the hatred of the women. But this meant nothing to her. The whole world existed only in her little cottage, in Elo's arms, in their nights. Now he'd fish and she'd clean and tidy, cook him tasty meals with the most amazing herbs and leaves. The way to a man's heart was through his stomach, some granny had told her and Vanda hadn't forgotten. Looking after someone brought her pleasure, especially when that someone was Elo.

Vanda had grown up on her own. Early in her early teens her mother and father had passed away suddenly from some illness, which no-one recognised. Vanda buried them, she got into her father's boat and rowed a long time. Then she released the oars to rock freely in the rowlocks and let the waves carry her. She didn't remember how long she spent out at sea. One morning she woke with a sharp pain in her shrivelled tummy. She couldn't remember when she had eaten last. She picked one of the lures and began to unwind it. The thin nylon wire immediately twitched in her fingers and she quickly drew it in. The silver bodies of a dozen fish glittered in the first rays of the sun and flapped on the bottom of the boat. Vanda unhooked them and again let out the line with its hooks into the water. And it twitched in her fingers again. She was carried away by the rich harvest, she filled the two boxes, grabbed the oars and set off for the shore. The pain in her soul died down and as long as she was fishing she hardly felt it. From that time on she began to go out into the sea every morning before dawn and to return with boxes full. She sold most of her catch to the holiday-makers, who were passing quickly through the village, and only kept a little for herself. Just as much as she needed.

The fishermen realized that, however much by chance, she always happened upon large shoals of fish, they waited to see where she went in the morning, and only then entered the sea, and circled her with their boats. They threw out their snares or nets, but they never matched her catch.

Vanda grew up and received several marriage proposals. She refused them all. She lived with an obscure feeling that she would experience something different. She didn't just want to get married because that was the accepted thing to do, she didn't want to be like the characterless messy women from the village. Her body was awakening, her thoughts hovered somewhere far away in the unknown and the air around her quivered in anticipation. The men felt it but did not dare approach her cottage. They knew that she'd taken out her father's old gun and was holding it ready under her arm day and night.

For several years in a row at the end of Spring, Vanda stirred three spoons of salt and one spoon of flour with a little water, she mixed the dough, baked it in a tin and before going to bed, she ate the little roll. She remembered from her Granny that whoever gave her a glass of water in her dream would be her future husband. But every time only one hand would bring her water, a male hand with soft pale hairs on it, and it would quickly be withdrawn. Vanda saw neither the man's figure nor his face. And the next year she baked the roll again, threw herself on the bed and closed her eyes. She fell asleep quickly, she was tortured by thirst and again the pale downy hand appeared and offered her a glass. Vanda took it, but didn't put it to her lips, and she tried to follow the hand so as to see the man's face. In her impatience she let the glass slip and it shattered into a thousand tiny pieces at her feet.

Elo appeared in the village and began fishing with the men. Vanda saw him on the quay and, goodness knows why, she felt her heart turn over several times and freeze in her throat. She stopped and she couldn't take her eyes off his hands – strong manly hands, but very white with soft golden hairs on them. Hands very different from the swarthy hairy hands of the men from the village.

Vanda was the first to sense the enmity which built up around Elo. One night she went to Elo's hut and from a distance noticed the men's silhouettes which circled around. The next night Vanda brought her gun and took up position close to the hut. A little later three of the fishermen approached without seeing her. Vanda took two steps forward, stood in a bright spot lit by the moon, and pointed the gun at the first man's stomach. The men noticed her only now, they stopped dumbstruck and waited. Vanda didn't say a word but didn't shift the muzzle. The silence thickened around them. The first man took a step back, turned and left. The other two followed him. Vanda waited for them to depart. She went back to her post, sat down with her back pressed into a tree. She stayed like this until the sky began to lighten. Then she shouldered the gun and set off for her cottage. She knew that during the day no-one would dare attack Elo. That's how it was here, nothing happened at daytime, if someone had to do something, he did it at night.

Vanda got home, threw herself on the bed and the whole day she slept like a log. Only in the afternoon, when the other boats returned she went out into the sea. She came back before sunset and in the night once more took up position in front of the hut. But neither that night nor in the following nights did anyone dare pass by. The word had spread that Vanda was guarding the newcomer with the gun they feared.

LYUDMILA ANDROVSKA

Right from the beginning of their life together Vanda realized that Elo possessed an inner strength that the other men lacked. She didn't spend too much time thinking about this, but when dark thoughts began to affect her ever more frequently and Elo kept her continually on edge with his infrequent presence, Vanda realized that this was the horrible strength of destructiveness. Slowly and furtively it flattened her remembered fine expectations of the unknown, destroyed her girlish dreams one by one, poisoned her nights, it even deprived her of the will to continue her life with this man. At first glance Elo didn't do anything, he carried on living as before, exchanging glances and smiles with other women, sometimes didn't come home at night and he'd answer her questions with a furtive smile and silence. He showed her that even if he were with her today, tomorrow he could quit. Or he could stay. He didn't know himself.

One morning Vanda watched how he was going down to the quay and realized that she didn't want him to come back any more. It was then she understood that the dark forces of destruction had begun to seep into her, somewhere inside in the very depths of her soul. She tried to suppress them to return them to her subconscious. Something stirred in her, pressured her from inside and stopped her breath. It happened exactly when the desire to kill was strong in her, but the creation of new life had begun. She didn't know whether to rejoice or cry. Confused, Vanda turned in on herself, she stopped cleaning the cottage and cooking her tasty meals. Elo didn't notice. He carried on in his own way, but once he realized the change in her, he began to hang out in their house and nervously circle his wife. Indifferent to everything, Vanda stayed wrapped up in herself.

Elo understood only when her tummy began to swell. Destruction exploded within him in all its fearsome force, and easily swept away the previous peaceful days and the balance which he'd won. Truth to tell, when he saw that Vanda was not trying to control him, Elo got tired and began to behave normally. He liked the life of the fishermen,

CHAOS

his interaction with the sea steadied him and calmed the chaos within him. With her slightly boyish behaviour, Vanda reminded him of his big sister and awakened a slight nostalgia. But when he saw her swelling belly, Elo felt trapped, suffocated by the long forgotten memory of the sticky plaintive love of his mother and he shuddered as if from a touch of slime. And one day he disappeared.

Vanda didn't notice his running away. She was used to his escapades and expected that one day or another he'd come back with his head dropped a little and an oily smile. She even liked the rest this gave her. Her joie de vivre returned, she got down to cleaning and tidying the house again, she made it shine, she filled it with flowers and for the first time for a long time she cooked. Only then did she feel a warm wave rise in her throat and she gently put her hands over her belly. She'd needed time to get used to the change. And now she accepted it. At the same time as the thickening of her body, a maternal feeling awoke in her. Then she realized how much she missed Elo. She counted the number of days in her head and it dawned on her that he'd been gone nearly a month. She set out to walk round the village and secretly look at the women, she observed them carefully, counted them, and in the end worked out with whom he'd run away. She took out her old gun with which she'd once guarded him, shouldered it and set out into the forest.

In three days Vanda returned, pointing the gun at Elo who was walking in front of her with head hung down, blackened with smoke and drawn.

That night Vanda lay in his arms, and in the morning she woke up on her own in the bed again. She gave a deep sigh, put away the gun and tried to forget him. But how would she forget him when his child was kicking in her womb. And when she went to give birth, she yearned for him to be with her, to hold her hand, and to rejoice in their baby...

No-one believed that Vanda would survive. And they'd felt sorry for the baby. But after about a month, she returned hale and hearty with a sturdy plump baby. Through the village the rumour spread from who knows where that it had been cut from her womb. The women began inquisitively to hang around the fence of Vanda's cottage and to peer in with half an eye. Vanda made out that she didn't notice them and busied herself in the yard, as she cradled her tummy. And several times she would water the place where she had planted the walnut.

Her difficult birth made her visit Granny Dushka more often and help her with the village mothers-to-be. The Granny was old and was pleased that she had a young helper and she'd be leaving her skills in dependable hands.

5

The girl Elo had run off with, returned to the village, with her tummy blown up in front of her. Vanda saw her and understood that she'd been deserted in her turn.

At the same time as her return, the wife of Peter the Tree disappeared. She was a woman with a youth and beauty, rarely encountered in the village. In her black eyes there burnt some kind of strange flame, which became all the stronger from the time her husband got to drinking. They called him the Tree because he'd always be carrying a piece of wood in his hands and be whittling it. He'd carved the beams for all the barns in the village with fabulous figures, strangely beautiful in their way. None of the fishermen appreciated his art, they wondered about his sanity, they cut out the beams, burnt them and in their place put new ones, supposedly thicker and stronger. Peter the Tree watched how they burnt and destroyed his work, he gathered up his chisels and set off for the pub. This happened more and more often until in the end there was no need for him to go there because now he never left. And no wonder that he didn't notice his wife's disappearance.

Perhaps only Vanda sensed where the Tree's wife had gone. She sensed it with that female intuition which men have wondered at over centuries. Again a wave of fury and destruction broke over her, but she managed it when she looked at her son. He was a white plump baby with golden down on his head and big blue eyes. She named him Mavri, after her father. She immediately saw the resemblance with Elo and an obscure fear grew within her whether he too would carry his father's destructive force. That's why in time when Mavri wanted to go on his own to the city and to leave his wife and five children here, Vanda threw all the energy she still had after all these years to stop him. But the chaos within him, the same chaos which sent his father off in different directions, pushed him to the other side. It was then Vanda understood that whether he stayed in the village with his family or he set out for somewhere on his own, the force had dug deep into him and was shoving towards even greater destruction, which would sweep away everything barring his path.

Elo's second child was born practically into Vanda's hands. Pale and beautiful, he bore a resemblance to her son. They were brothers after all, just from different mothers. The father had marked them with his stamp of chaos.

Turned blue and reduced by pain, the mother passed away quietly. The birth had been difficult. Frightened, with trembling hands, Granny Dushka tried to stop the blood from the torn insides. Vanda crossed herself with frozen fingers and whispered, "Lord God, don't take her...I didn't want this, Lord...She's not to blame..."

With the other hand she pressed the baby to her breasts.

The mother opened her darkened eyes, sunk like two holes into her face, looked at her child and life returned to her dying body with a new strength. Her chest was wheezing, sweat covered her face, she tried to stretch her hand towards the baby and exhausted by the effort she again collapsed. Life was leaving her, her nose sharpened, her skin became grey, her eyes opened one last time, fixed on the child and everything was repeated.

At last Granny Dushka could stand this endless pain no longer, she turned to Vanda and screamed at her, "Take that child out so she can die in peace!"

Vanda got up as if sleepwalking and went out, hugging the little body. She set out straight for her home and put the new child into Mavri's crib.

CHAOS

Straight after her departure, the mother left this world for good.

When the next day the bell rang out its slow dirge for her, the wooden coffin was followed only by Granny Dushka and Vanda, holding the two children.

After the burial they returned to the church and christened the new-born Belinko. In one day they managed a funeral and a christening.

Vanda took the child in and for the first months she breastfed him along with her son. And when the two hungry mouths had sucked her dry, Granny Dushka took over the young one. By now she couldn't help as a midwife, her hands shook and the death of Belinko's mother had scared her.

From then on Vanda wore a black cardigan, thereafter she accepted as fairly natural her emerging future life in the village and quite naturally as well they began to call her Granny Vanda. And she was so young…Young you say, she'd smile sadly, look out at the sea, and bitter lines would be engraved around her mouth. Youth disappeared along with the man who had sown discord in her soul and left her on her own. And Vanda would grimace with a slightly strange smile, when she thought of her youthful dreams, her obscure feeling that she'd go through something different. And to tell the truth the experience was the exactly same as in her dream. The hand which for a moment offered her the glass of water and then quickly drew back. The hand with soft golden down. Elo's hand. He'd got her with child and he'd left. He'd taken away her love. He'd left her Mavri only. And she turned towards the place where she'd planted the walnut, which was growing simultaneously with her son.

The green stalk was already showing when Mavri took his first steps, and she made a little fence around the fragile tree, so the child wouldn't trample it. Because she'd planted it for his life.

Just then at early dawn, as he lurched back from the pub, Peter the Tree found a strange basket made of twigs, and in it a small package, wrapped in a blanket was moving and uttering sounds.

Peter the Tree was rooted to the spot and grunted in shock. He thought it was from drinking, he pinched himself and rubbed his eyes, but the basket stayed on the spot and the package suddenly let out a cry. Peter lost his wits entirely, but the steady wailing of the baby quickly sobered him up and he grabbed the basket and set off for Granny Dushka.

In her turn the old woman sent it to Vanda, hadn't she taken on being the midwife and she would know best who might have enough milk for yet another baby.

Once she'd seen the thin blonde hair, Vanda immediately knew whose baby this was, and Elo's confused soul was gazing at her through the still clouded blue eyes.

"How will we christen her?" she asked.

Peter the Tree shrugged his shoulders in bewilderment.

"Eh, as you're the one looking after her, let her have your name," Vanda suggested and Peter just nodded his head.

And on the same day in the church, Vanda had the foundling female, mother unknown, baptized with the name Petra, whom later the village would call Homeless.

6

Mavri had long ago parted with his mother, made his home and brought a wife to it, who bore him five children. Five boys with fair tousled hair and eyes as blue as the sea. Unruly, restless, confused souls.

Vanda behaved towards her daughter-in-law with ill-concealed envy and secret jealousy. She too would have given birth to five or ten children from a man whom she loved, to see him repeated both five and ten times, to feel him so many times inside her, to bring him to life, to build him up. And at least for the short time of creation for him to be faithful to her through his children. And after that she would have to live through separation from each of them again and every time she'd suffer an extraction from her own flesh. And five wounds would be left in her heart, ten bleeding wounds which would never heal. But in spite of this it was worthwhile to bestow life, to give birth again and again to the man she loved. In all his personal variations and to sculpt him. It was worth her being born again to experience all this.

The walnut stem grew twice as long as the necks of Mavri and Granny Vanda, but she still cared for it. She'd water it, dig up the earth around it. And when the weather grew warm, she'd take out a chair, under its shade, strip from her back her habitual black cardigan and slowly begin to unstitch it.

"Don't stay in the walnut shade without a cardigan, Granny Vanda," some woman shouted, come to peep through her fence, just so as to see from afar what she was up to.

LYUDMILA ANDROVSKA

"I know. I know," the old woman waved an arm. She knew very well that however hot it was, if you sit under a walnut, you have to be dressed. But how could she explain to this woman that this walnut was not like others, it wasn't run-of-the-mill, it was her walnut, it was the life of her son and it would protect her, under its shade nothing bad would happen to her. She could not explain to this ordinary woman, that's why she just shook her head and continued to take the cardigan apart. And every stitch she undid was a moment from the life of the village, from the life of every person here, who had cried first in her hands. In the black stitches the history of the deserted house on the cliff top was preserved, forgotten by the fishermen for so long. But Granny Vanda would not forget it. Her memory was the memory of the village. Here she had knitted Elo's advent, the nights when she'd protected his hut with gun in hand. Here was Mavri's birth, and after him the birth of two other children, and their growing up. Mavri, Belinko and Petra never learnt about their blood ties, and the village folk had forgotten this a long time ago. They knew that Mavri was Elo's son, but they hadn't thought at all about Belinko's appearance, and for them it was as if Petra had fallen out of the sky, without any connection with the village. Her name was only linked with Peter the Tree, and afterwards she only put them in mind of the nights in the barns. They found no link with Elo. Actually they'd forgotten about him long ago, he'd left them no memory, he didn't plant a tree, didn't build a house, came and went like a casual wayfarer, a man with no past or future... A man with no root.

Here the bell was sounding and it rang in every stitch and loop.

Here too the final days of Granny Dushka were knitted. The old woman looked after Belinko with the love that only solitary folk can give. She brought him up as a quiet, biddable child, and when he grew up she gave him a towel, in which she'd bundled up a little money and she helped him choose a kind good-natured wife. The old woman had managed to see him settled like all the others, and only then she

CHAOS

peacefully closed her eyes. Belinko and his wife buried her, then nine days later arranged a memorial and immediately after that he left for an unknown destination. His wife remained on her own in Granny Dushka's little house, astonished, driven out of her mind by her husband's running away, which had come to her like a thunderbolt from the clear sky.

Much time had flowed since then, but nothing was heard of Belinko, nor did he send any news. He'd simply left everything, hunted out by the dark confusion of his father's blood. Maybe one day he would return, but his wife decided not to wait in vain but to build her life without him. She straightened the house, furnished it with one bed, one table, one chair – a home for a solitary person. And then she began to travel. In her short periods of return, she'd look round the cottage to see if anyone had come, but she always found it as she had left it. As though Belinko had never been there.

The father's blood has its say in him, Granny Vanda thought and crossed herself fearfully, if only Mavri doesn't inherit it. And she'd knit her fear into the black cardigan as a spell.

Now she was unravelling it, stitch by stitch, second by second, fate by fate. The ball in her hands grew, it was swelling as if pregnant with life, her hands could not hold it, like she could not hold life itself.

Then she took two thick needles and knitted everything from the beginning. And the histories came back again, Elo turned up, he went away again, the wife of the Sailor stood high on the cliff, old Krayan began again to build his big house, Granny Dushka closed her eyes and the bell rang slowly and sadly, the babies passed through Vanda's hands. Everything was turning in an endless circle, knitted in black stitches and fixed in the memory.

The fishermen carefully followed Granny Vanda's knitting. They were young men, who were still crying in their baby cots when Elo came to the village. They did not know how Vanda protected their house and their love with her father's gun. They only knew her as Granny Vanda, sitting under the walnut tree, knitting or unstitching her eternal black cardigan. They knew that once the cardigan was knitted, autumn was now passing and winter would start soon.

That's when Mavri would come to his mother's garden, he'd climb the tree and begin to beat it. He'd gather the walnuts, stretch out his hands and begin to divide them – one nut to he left, then ten to the right. The left hand pile grew slowly, scarcely noticeable, while the right hand pile got big, as though it would fill the entire yard. Mavri would bring a sack from somewhere and tip the big pile into it.

Granny Vanda would watch him, without saying anything, she'd wait for him to leave, then she'd gather the small pile inside, put on her new black cardigan and bring the chair back into the house.

After one or two days the weather would darken, storms would blow up and cold rains would fall.

7

The forest squeezed the village from three sides. The cottages scarcely rose above the ground, low, with tiny windows, they wound amongst the trees, like the folk who were crammed inside them. The men were dark, withdrawn, heavy in their step and their speech, and the women were grey, emaciated. Over them clothes hung shapeless and colourless. Throughout their lives they struggled on the one side with the sea that fed them and on the other, with the forest which warmed them in the winter. Within the village, besides with themselves, they lad a fight with the mice. They laid traps and poison, but the little rodents continued to dig holes through the walls and to walk about carefree everywhere. They were small brownish field mice which at one time had turned up, simultaneously with the arrival of Elo, who knows how they'd happened there and survived so many generations in these wooded areas by the sea,

In the afternoon the men returned from fishing, left their meagre catch with their wives and went into the forest for wood. They wanted to enlarge their houses, so that there'd be room for them and their children, and for their children's children one day. But in spite of their efforts, their houses remained still small and tight, and their wives wanted babies.

In the evening the men would return, weighed down with exhaustion, ate the rewarmed meal and stretched out their bodies, sucked dry by the salty air. Their wives set their backs to their husbands, to warm up, and they gave way to sleep, colourless and grainy like the wattle and daub walls of their houses.

But before returning to their homes the men would make their way to Granddad Nacho's pub, to down a few glasses, which relaxed their bodily movements and the stiffness of their souls. Then life didn't seem to them so grey, or their wives so ugly. And on Saturday nights they drank a hot black substance which Granddad Nacho had brought in recently and would sell it for one price in the day and another at night, three times lower than the morning.

"What is this, Uncle Nacho?" the men asked.

"Coffee," the old man declared proudly, pleased by the attention. "When you want to sleep in the morning, it will wake you up and keep you alert throughout the day.

But the men were poor and drank the coffee in the evening. The whole night afterwards they couldn't sleep a wink and could hardly see from exhaustion. That's why they decided to only drink coffee on Saturday evenings, so they could sleep on the Sunday.

The women got used to the fact that on Saturday nights the men returned awake and full of energy. The men lay next to them, but the adrenalin weighed uneasily and stopped them sleeping. So they turned and tried to sink in between their wives' contorted bones. But the wives would push them away, because they didn't want to be pregnant, the men would jump up and go out and make for barn after barn, seeking Homeless Petra. And when they found her, into her sterile womb they shot out all these dreams for children, grandchildren and great-grandchildren, because of whom on the next day, they'd again enter the forest to extend their houses. They'd set out with relieved bodies and depressed spirits, robbed and sorrowful.

8

As silent as all the others, Mavri differed from them only with his blond hair and his blue eyes. He was sturdy and well built like his father, but also like his mother – Granny Vanda – his hair began to turn white early. The white curls mixed in with the blond hair and were not noticed. His blond moustache was not unkempt but evenly cut and every morning he shaved his cheeks smooth from the golden hair on them. His home-woven shirt always bleached to blue, like the snow which lasted up on the mountain all the way to the following winter. And however he exhausted himself during the day, he never turned his back on his wife.

Close to Mavri's house, in the centre of the village, by the low-lying church, there was a bell tower – the only tall object here – and source of the people's pride. Early in the morning even before sunrise, the bell would awaken the stunted houses.

First of all, the footsteps of the men passed through the church yard, hurrying towards the little quay. They'd untie the boats and set out into the sea. And after the sun had swum up above the endless blue waters, the children jumped out as well. Gripping huge slices of bread and with grubby cheeks, they flocked together, yelling, shrieking through the tall grass of the church yard. The old verger didn't cut it on purpose, and let it grow the whole summer. He knew how much the children enjoyed playing in it. Later the children's bare feet would transfer to the cliff.

At midday the bell rang again. Then the women would emerge, make their way to the Granddad Yovan's baking oven, and holding the hot fluffy bread they'd gather the hungry little ones.

Just as they didn't know from what unknown roads Granddad Nacho bought the magical drinks, which lifted them three feet from the ground, so no-one knew where and how Granddad Yordan found flour and yeast, and how he transported them here. This was the old pair's big secret. With Granddad's bread the salted dry fish could be swallowed more easily. If it wasn't for him and his bakery, they'd have died of hunger.

"And so we've still got something to dump in the shitter in the morning," Granddad Nacho would say with his dark humour.

But he too, like everyone, sent out his old wife for bread, they'd eat the pair of them, and in the afternoon, like the other old folk, he'd take a crafty puff in the yard. The Grannies clattered their pots and pans in the kitchen.

The village quietened down in expectation.

In the late afternoon, when the men returned from the sea and entered the forest, the bell would ring again. From the stunted houses, the old folk crept out, who'd been young in Elo's time. Holding a cushion under their arms, they slowly pieced their way over the cobble stones, holding on to one another. They'd line up the cushions on the low wall under the bell tower, squatted down and would sit for hours.

At this time summer holiday makers would arrive at the port. Some of the men stayed behind to sell from their anyway quite small catch. The holiday makers bought the fish and left for the sun-soaked beaches.

The children circled round, for them these people were coming from some other world and carried with them something of that unfamiliar spirit of adventure and strangeness, for which they dreamt a lot. And they gazed at their clothes, sniffed at them with inquisitive little noses and with a simulated arrogance, they'd walk past their

CHAOS

children. Children for whom the world was no secret, unlike for themselves.

Once a half naked kid in bright shorts shouted out, "Fy, you lot here are living like in Atlantis!"

The children gaped at him in surprize, not knowing whether to be insulted and give him a beating or to turn up their noses. Pride prevented asking what he had meant.

"You're cut off from all the world," the lad continued, explaining as though he'd read their thoughts. "Atlantis was a continent, which no-one has seen... and as for you, no-one sees you. You are frozen like in a silent picture."

"What's that?" Mavri's youngest son asked, he'd inherited his curiosity from the root of his Granddad Elo.

His question simply provoked a scornful smile from the unknown lad.

"And where is this continent?" the little boy asked again and at the same moment doubled up. His older brother had come up behind him and whacked the back of his head to shut him up.

"Nowhere. Atlantis is extinct. The ocean swallowed it up."

"We're not extinct" Mavri's eldest son shouted out and he shook his head. "The sea will never swallow us!" And he squeezed his little brother's neck, before he could ask anything else and turned his back.

And the other lads hurried to be the first to turn their backs on this unknown learned kid and like everyone else made towards the cliff. They climbed up the narrow path, one after the other, passing Granny Vanda, who sitting under the walnut, was as ever knitting her black cardigan. The old woman smiled at them as stitch by stitch she knitted the lives of every one of them. She knew them all, wasn't she the first to take them on, before their mothers saw them. And the boys blushed, greeted her abruptly, dropped their heads in embarrassment and shivers went up and down their spines. As if Granny Vanda did not know their most hidden thoughts and desires, and their future fates. The children quickened their steps and continued further up, where the path had been trodden down only by their little feet. They climbed up, went round the little house on the summit, then they sat on the rock above the sea and fixed their eyes on the horizon. They were silent and without looking at one another, embarrassed by their words and thoughts which they distorted, they exchanged opinions on the beautiful female holidaymakers. They didn't look at all like their mothers, these beautiful women with their colourful revealing dresses and their fair hair cascading to their sunburnt shoulders. They'd only heard of such a woman in their village from Granny Vanda, but they had not seen her. And there was no way they could have seen her, she had lived here, above the sea, some time, a long time ago, when the oldies had been young lads like them.

And the only one who compared in beauty with the holidaymakers was Homeless Petra.

Once the lads were playing in the secluded inlet between the cliffs, when they saw a siren swimming towards them through the clear calm water. The lads hid behind the rocks and held their breath from curiosity and with beating hearts. The siren's skin shone white like sea foam, her long golden hair flowed out behind her and a thousand droplets spilled out like glitter dust. The boys were silent, stifled, their hearts already jumping into their throats.

Homeless Petra noticed their widened eyes behind the rocks, but pretended not to see them, she just quietly laughed to herself. The same boys were looking at her, whose fathers came to her in the night, the same boys, who in one or two years would be looking for her panting in the barns. And Petra slowly came out of the water, stopped, turned in every direction towards their dumbfounded looks, and revealed in detail all that in time they would possess. With an easy gait she walked on the gravel beach, looked around one more time, catching out of the corner of her eye, their excited looks and was left satisfied with the effect. Then she stopped in front of a little bundle, they had not

CHAOS

noticed, bent down, lifted some rag and put it on. And in front of their eyes, rounded in astonishment, she turned into Homeless Petra. She laughed once more to herself and left.

Many times after that her beautiful naked body returned to the boys in their dreams, her golden hair unfurled in the water, the easy movements of her long legs... Many years after that the former boys, now men, would be comparing every woman he met in life with her – the first – and no-one would pass the comparison. It would be difficult for these boys.

But now they didn't realize this, they looked on, breathless, and tried to swallow the hearts stuck in their throats.

And later when their parents set aside something for Homeless Petra, the boys would furtively pop into her bundle something from their treasures – a beautiful shell or a sparkling stone, found on the shore. And later they'd go to the church yard and sit close to the old folk, as they'd furtively look out in hopes of seeing her. They knew that Petra came by to look up the old verger. The pair would share their loneliness and meagre provisions.

No-one in the village knew the verger's secret, almost as old as him. They didn't even suspect that for years he'd pledged his life to Vanda. He was quite young when Vanda protected her home and honour with a gun, then he found out about her rejection of so many lads, and himself lacked the courage to ask her. He took her marriage to Elo hard, and so entered the church. He attended the baptism of her three children and with some deep intuition, inherent in women only, he sensed the link between them. Later he poured out all of his propensity to love and care for someone over Petra, she was the one most in need of this. But Petra avoided his attention, came from time to time, and took care not to meet his eye. And if this happened involuntarily, she'd drop her eyes. She had the feeling that the verger valued her soul as no-one else's. Her troubled soul was the only thing that remained hers alone and she allowed no-one to peer into it.

And the old folk expected the verger to unravel forgotten memories. He was a good listener. He's squat down next to them, sometimes smiling and shaking his head in thought. He never spoke but came alive in their stories as if he too had been with them there. In that faraway time. He'd smoke one or two cigarettes, smile sadly and leave through the church yard along with his loneliness. Without him the incidents lost their flavour, the talk became lethargic and gradually died down. The old folk stopped talking. Bitter sighs lurked and poisoned the falling darkness.

Then Granddad Nacho would begin to talk. In his quiet voice he'd tell about the black formal suit, bought from the town, when he was still young. He'd keep it separate from his other clothes in the wardrobe and every spring, he'd take it out, clean it, sprinkle it with naphthalene and put it back. He'd put aside a sheet as well – linen with a lace fringe. Granny Vanda had woven it at the time.

"I've liked it since then," he said, "and kept it safe."

"And my granny made preparations," Granddad Yovan sucked at his cigarette and shook his white head. "Like a dowry, she'd fixed up a chest. But when you've gone, it's still there..."

Granddad Nacho didn't agree and pulled angrily at his yellowing moustaches.

It became quite dark. The verger rang the bell and the old folk's faltering feet took them back to the darkened village. The Verger took a candle, collected what was left of the food into the church, took it into his little room under the bell tower, laid it out on the table and waited for Homeless Petra to come.

9

Homeless Petra didn't know her mother. Her memory from earliest childhood was her perpetually drunken father, who every time he set out for the pub, would take away something from their home. In the end they slept flat out on the wooden floor.

Petra didn't know why her father drank and never tried to understand. She only saw his infrequent unsteady homecomings and his clouded eyes, which sometimes fixed on her for a long time. He'd look at her in such a way that his eyes would run with tears.

Granny Vanda had secretly hoped that through looking after the child, Peter the Tree would stop drinking. And, truth to tell, it started off well, but Peter the Tree realized who this child abandoned in front of his door was. Over time he thought ever more often about his wife's running away and the presence of Petra was a continual reminder.

Once Peter the Tree did not come back. In his place some strangers came, looked over the two rooms, wrote over some papers, and a neighbour took the little girl's hand and led her away. Then Petra realized that she could no longer return home. But she understood that she could live in every barn in the village, without anyone chasing her away. She understood that even though no-one paid her any attention, in every barn, supposedly by chance, there'd always be something to eat, some hardy item of clothing or a thick rug to cover her.... And in spite of this Petra realized that there's nothing nicer than to have a home.

Petra did not know that the village saw her like their own dodgy consciences. When she was left without a home, every fisherman suggested to his wife that they should take her in.

"One child more or less makes no difference," said all of the husbands.

But the wives reacted as one.

"We've got nowhere to put our own children, and how would we feed yet another one…" And they bristled like eagles, protecting their nest of chicks.

Was it poverty that made them reject the little girl, left on her own, was it fear that they'd deprive their own children from their already meagre portions. Or some deep intuition, which predicted that the girl would soon be a woman and would turn into a threat.

The fishermen were frustrated with their wives, but did not dare to undertake anything without their agreement. In time when they stood in a queue before Homeless Petra they were grateful to them.

In spite of their decisiveness, the women were not convinced that they'd made the right choice. And this doubt made them put out food, rugs and clothes, in the barns, to redeem their guilt. But that didn't stop them choosing only old ugly clothes, so that wearing them Petra's beauty would fade away. So that the homeless girl would become grey and merge into the village female crowd.

When she saw her passing somewhere close by dressed in her rags, Granny Vanda could not hold back: "A beautiful horse stands out even from under a ragged blanket…"

And if her daughter-in-law was around she'd say it in a loud voice for her to hear.

"Yeah but that's only true for horses!" her daughter-in-law would interject spitefully and hurry to leave.

Granny Vanda would laugh to herself.

10

The only big house in the village belonged to the Krayan family – a tall white building, of two stories with thick strong walls, as stable as their owner – old Krayan.

In his restless youth Krayan's son took to the high road, supposedly for a long time, but he returned suddenly when no-one expected him. With him he brought a woman, whose figure was expanding suspiciously quickly. And so they raised a wedding.

The old man looked thoughtfully at his daughter-in-law's blown up proportions, and then switched his look towards the house that was shrinking before his eyes. A house like all the other houses in the village, made from wattle and daub and wood, with two small rooms. And he rolled up his sleeves. He got his relatives and neighbours to help and the new home grew quickly, alongside the young wife's tummy.

And one night through Vanda's hands Teo entered the white world, in a big empty room, bright and white, with the smell of bricks, quicklime, damp and something else, warm and nice, breathing security and protection, the motherly embrace.

The old man waited for the child to grow, to walk, and learn his first words, and only then to set to finishing the terrace which he wanted to have on the second floor.

He finished it when the second baby was on the way. It was spacious with a single support beam beneath its outer corner. As they were working in the garden the beam snapped, and before the daughter-in-law could cry out, the terrace slab broke off and crushed old Krayan, leaving only his head, feet and outstretched hands visible. The old man was finished on the spot, with a snapped back bone and crushed body, and the young woman went into premature labour and followed him a few days later.

Busy with the burials and her sorrow, old Krayanka paid attention to nobody.

Teo bounded about the garden, repeating the words he'd learnt – "Granddad", "house"... Only he didn't know "Mummy", but now there was no-one to explain it to him. His father didn't notice him, he hung around in silence, and something still tugged him to the place where the slab had fallen. And throughout all this time, the slow drawn out ring of the bell carried over the village..

In the hot summer days, on the broken slab, a snake began to appear. It would sun itself, lying out on the rough edge.

Teo still remembered the first time when he saw it – it had taken to the jagged edges of the broken slab with its flexible body, it was lying like a smooth straight brown tape. The sun broke on the miniature scales and each of them glowed differently – gold-brown, red-brown, green-brown, silver-brown...Every nuance pulsed, throbbed and made the cold body of the snake warm, seducing a boyish hand to stroke it.

Teo did not remember how he climbed to the second floor, how he got to the edge of the terrace and reached his hand towards the hundred living brown colours. . The only memory that remains is his father's shouting from below, brandishing a stone in his hand, and his Grandma Krayanka's hand which stopped him with a scream: "Do you want to kill your father?" her voice split the air and echoed everywhere. "Don't you know that a snake in the house is the soul of its first owner?"

These words made the stone fall on the ground and Teo's hand to rest on the edge. At the same moment, the snake crawled over the rough surface, then over the child's hand, as if to caress it, and disappeared as suddenly as it had appeared. Teo was not scared when

CHAOS

the long snake body stretched itself vertebrae after vertebrae over his skin. He knew his Granddad wouldn't harm him.

And his Granny and Dad watched him from below, frozen.

That made his father think again about making another parapet. He was in no hurry to start, but stood in the garden and gazed for hours at the second floor... He looked day after day, month after month, year after year.

"I'll go to the town for a significant spell... When I come back I'll do it." He nodded at the terrace.

After a month they brought his cold dead body back.

The bell again rang out its slow drawn out clang.

11

At this time the news spread that Belinko had divorced.

In the village they heard the word "divorce" for the first time. They needed time to get their heads round it, and in the end Granny Vanda explained it again. The old woman had a reason for knowing. Back then, a few years after Elo left, Vanda decided that it was right to have their separation documented. And so she went to the town for a second time. When she realized that she would have to go to the court along with Elo, to find him and bring him there, that they'd have to talk one against the other, she gave it up and quickly returned to the village. She decided that she wouldn't live with anyone else, so why was it necessary then?

When they learnt the meaning of the word the fishermen circled inquisitively around the home of Belinko's wife, they wondered if they could discuss the event, they thought, they looked, but it wasn't something you could see, touch or eat, so they soon forgot it. They were impressed by the fact that Belinko's wife was now free, same as though she hadn't married, this was unusual for them, she was married, she wasn't married… They looked at her, but they saw no change in her. She and Belinko had lived a long time separated, from when he tore off somewhere, there was no news of him, and whether he'd write down on paper that they were not together, it made little difference. And from outside, Belinko's wife had not changed. She remained the same. Sometimes evil spirits would take over her, she couldn't find room for herself and so the crash of breakage was heard, the clang of saucepans and trays being thrown about. Later they saw her wandering round the garden with her hair in a mess and unfastened clothes, she'd be tying up a bundle and setting off somewhere. To some neighbouring village, to her sister, was the answer she'd give to inquisitive questions from the fishermen's wives. The fishermen did not recall Belinko's wife to have had a sister, at least there not before Belinko left her, but they didn't think long over it. After a few days, she'd return, smiling and calm. Life ran on as always. Everything was forgotten till it happened again.

Only Granny Vanda understood what these evil spirits were. She knew that Belinko carried that destructive force, those dark whirlwinds within himself, inherited from his father, which freely invaded his wife's soul. It made no difference that they were separated by a document, the sediment had floated up from the depths of her subconscious and nothing could return it again, hidden in subterfuge.

The men had not paid goodness knows what attention to the news, and now had forgotten her almost entirely. Other worries squeezed them – the mice multiplied horribly. Only in Krayan's garden, they didn't pop up, perhaps because of the snake, whose presence provoked whispers in the village.

12

On one of these days the bell did not ring, either in the morning or at midday. The village fell quiet in surprize.

Only in the afternoon a muffled drawn out tolling was heard, echoing mournfully through the silenced houses, striking them and dying away. After that another tolling struck people in their frozen faces and it too had its say... And once more... Over the village a cry broke out, horrid and lonely, and it merged with the slow chimes of the bell.

They brought a coffin out of a house, covered in white linen. The men gathered together that day and no-one went out into the sea. They followed the white coffin, with heavy steps. Two tough men with greying moustaches supported an old woman dressed in black.

The sad procession passed through the churchyard, and cut a wide path through the long grass. The chiming of the bell reverberated for a long time afterwards. The next day the stamped down grass would yellow and dry out.

In the morning the stunted houses woke up to the vague foreboding that something had changed. People looked around and realized – through the yards cats were creeping, as scrawny and colourless as the village women. They drifted silently like shadows, with lowered heads and watchful eyes, and only meowed when they caught a mouse. There was a vague threat in their silence, which made the skin bristle in inexplicable horror. And despite shivering at their appearance, the men hid the traps and the poison, leaving the struggle with mice to the paws of the cats.

CHAOS

The verger had disappeared. He felt guilty, announcing death.

On this day too, the bell was ominously silent, but when it did not toll in the afternoon, the old folk took their cushions and made their way to the church yard. They squatted quietly on the low stonewall like utterly exhausted birds and lowered their whitened heads. Those same men were sitting underneath the bell tower, who had once aimed to beat Elo. The same women looked up towards the bell tower, who had once hemmed in Vanda with their jealousy. Men and women who were no longer young.

From time to time they dropped in a good word, for Granddad Yordan, might he rest in peace, and they shared their fear. Whose turn would it be next? And Granddad Yordan's old wife was not to be seen. She'd shut herself up in their little house, she was weeping silently and bending ever closer to the ground, to merge with it.

The bakery was deserted. There'd be no more bread. The women would be taking old wooden bread pans, but they didn't know where to get their hands on flour and yeast. Granddad Yordan had taken the secret with him.

"I want to be put next to Dad," said Granddad Nacho in the silence of the heavily falling dusk. "And Visha to be put beside me..."

No-one answered, or added anything.

Granddad Nacho sighed and looked upwards.

The bell was silent.

13

Granny Krayanka buried her son with the same manly spirit with which she'd previously coped with the deaths of her husband, her daughter-in-law along with the unborn child. And as previously, Granny Vanda helped her with washing the corpse and dressing it in new clothes.

"This is my fate," Granny Vanda thought, as she poured water over young Krayan's cold extremities "To be the first and last to wash them..."

And she swallowed her tears.

The next day old Krayanka could not get up from her bed. The old woman understood the reason and knew it would last a long time.

Teo was scared for her. He felt it with some vague sixth sense, and an even stronger fear took him over. He began to bring food to her little room at the end of the corridor, where there was just room to open the door and just two steps to get to the tall narrow iron bed.

"Come on, let's move you," Teo would say. "There are so many big bright rooms, all of them are for you, and you're curled up here."

Krayanka looked at him with her dry wrinkled eyes. How much he's grown, she checked him over and concluded that she could happily leave him on his own.

"They are for you," she'd answer quietly. "For you and your wife... I don't want to make them dirty."

Teo put the bowl at the head, sat down at the edge of the bed and took hold of the skinny bony hand.

CHAOS

"And something else..." Krayanka continued, "When you choose a wife, choose her by her hands. Her hands should be hot... They're lying to you, when they tell you that cold hands show a warm heart. A stove can't heat if its pipes are cold."

Teo tenderly stroked her hand. "Don't worry. Everything will all right..." He bent down towards her dry wrinkled cheek.

Krayanka felt how something was choking her throat and signalled with her eyes for him to leave. Teo shook his head in denial, lifted the pillow under her, took the bowl and as every other time began slowly and carefully to feed her. The old woman refused the food, she turned and pushed his hand away, but finally surrendered to his insistent care and ate a couple of spoonfuls.

Teo wanted to carry her outside, to sit under the warm sun, but her opposition was so pronounced that he gave up. He stayed a little longer with her and when he saw her eyes closing, he got up and left the room on tiptoe. Then the old woman opened her eyes, looked out at the closed door and two salty channels ran down her dried out face.

"Gather me in, more quickly, Lord," she whispered. "Take me, so he doesn't suffer and for it to go easier for me..."

And she refused to eat. In the beginning she tricked Teo into bringing her the food and leaving her to feed herself, then she'd throw it under the bed. In time Teo realized this and tried to feed her again, with a spoon only, but petty much failed. Krayanka declined quickly, but her healthy body did not want to give way, however weakened.

Teo cooked on his own, he made tasty light soups from herbs and brought them to his Granny warm and fragrant. She'd taken him into the forest from the earliest years and shown him what greenery could be taken for cooking, already she was preparing him for the days when he'd be left on his own. Later she'd shown the same things to Homeless Petra, the girl had an instinct for forest greenery, she'd pick them and take them to the village women.

Now Teo cooked these soups for his Granny, but old Krayanka pursed her lips like a child and turned her head away. Teo wondered what to do, he tried various tricks to get her to eat, but nothing helped.

One morning the bowl was again empty. Teo bent down and saw the soup spilled under the bed, like other times.

"What have you done again!" he yelled and anger welled up in him. "Don't you realize I can't take anymore!"

He collapsed on the end of the bed at her feet in futile anger and helplessness, ready to weep.

"Why are you shouting at me?" his Granny's voice quivered quietly.

Teo looked at her and saw her tear-filled eyes. He was overcome with pity for her, she was departing and he could barely control his nerves over some spilt soup. He moved further up the bed, stretched out a hand and stroked her head. Beneath his fingers he felt rough bumps. He looked carefully and under the thinning hair he saw blue-purple swellings.

"What is this?" he asked. Then he looked at the bowl left close to her head and understood. "What have you done?" his voice was shaking.

"I don't want you struggling with me," old Krayanka whispered. "I bashed and bashed, but I can't break this thick skull, I don't have enough strength." And she burst into tears.

Teo wept along with her, he hid his head in her shoulder. With horror he thought what would have happened, if the old woman had more strength and had managed to hit herself harder with the heavy clay bowl.

"Some morning, you'll come in and find me dead," his Granny continued in a quivering voice. "You shouldn't be scared of that, it will be better for you and for me it will be a rescue. It's high time for me to go."

CHAOS

Teo stayed with her the whole day and late into the evening, he waited for her to sleep and only then went to bed himself. In the morning he woke up early and hurried to go to her

Large green-black flies had appeared in the room. Teo brandished a big white towel in a futile attempt to chase them away.

Krayanka barely managed to lift her eyelids on his entering he room. He put the tray underneath her that he used for her toilet and when he extracted it, he just saw a tile-brown liquid. And he got scared...

His Granny twitched her fingers and took his hand. Yeo understood. He sat on the edge of the blanket and leant his head towards the scarcely trembling lips so he could catch her whispering.

"Marry..." the old woman was saying. "No-one should be left on their own. There's nothing more horrible than loneliness. Marry Homeless Petra. Every woman dreams of a home. And whoever has not had one, will be beholden to you all her life and grateful that you've given it to her."

Old Krayanka stopped talking, her head fell back, her fingers stiffened. Teo went out, he washed the tray, cleaned the house and tried to chase away a haunting premonition. Something irresistible pulled him to the little room and simultaneously pulled him back. Several times he opened the door to peek inside. Granny was sleeping as always with mouth wide open and head swept back. Teo sighed in relief and closed the door quietly. In late afternoon he was seized by some doubt, he couldn't sleep the whole day, he was so restless, he went into her room and stepped quickly to her, took her hand and called to her quietly.

"Granny!"

Krayanka didn't answer, she didn't even quiver. Her sharpened nose stuck out as if it was a fake fixed on her face. Her hand got icy cold in his fingers. In the air above her the big green-black flies circled, and one of them was crawling on her tongue in the wide open mouth. Teo chased it off, sat for a last time on the edge of the bed, grabbed the cold bony hand and bent his head over her.

He stayed like this a long time, then he stood up, wiped his face and left to call Granny Vanda.

The bell tolled with the same drawn out clang and the village trembled again. A small procession set out from Krayanka's bright white house.

14

Belinko came back.

He returned to the surprize of the whole village, the men, the women and Granny Vanda most of all, she who knew the chaos inside him. He returned to the astonishment of his former wife, who was more amazed by his return than ever by his running off. And she didn't know whether to be pleased or not, whether to stay in Granny Dushka's house or to pack her bags and seek shelter elsewhere. Her brother had married almost straight away after her and there was no room in her parents' house. It was so tight there, that her brother and sister-in-law were holding back from having kids. She stayed, closed up in the kitchen in amazement and fear and waited for Belinka to turn up. But he didn't, only from time to time some neighbour passed by to bring her news. And from this news, Belinko's former wife's crazed spirit reared up and made her blood boil with fury. O one day she'd pay Belinko back.

The fishermen were left with the vague feeling that Belinko had appeared simultaneously with the cats. They barely recognized him, he had changed so much. They didn't look at him either, they couldn't take their eyes off the woman who walked beside him. A different woman, not like theirs, tall, melting, and whichever way you turned her, she had a rounded shape, and not just jutting bones. Her loosened bright hair shone like the sun sparks which played on the sea waves and the leaves on the trees.

Both old and young followed her, struck dumb, their hearts thumping. Somewhere far back in the old folk's memories, something was trying to bring up the image of at least one more woman like her, but it was so unclear, that they gave up on straining their faded memories. Even if that woman existed, she was from a long, long time ago, and this one now was warm, and alive, before their eyes, and her laughter made their old hearts quiver. And they continued to not take their eyes off Belinko's new woman.

Belinko took her into the forest and began making a hut. The whole village hurried to help them and in one day their forest home was ready.

Granny Vanda came as well, she walked all around the hut, and secretly crossed herself. She remembered another hut, pretty much like this one, but further into the forest and many, many years ago. In that other hut Belinko was conceived. From there, gun in hand, Vanda had driven his father.

"How everything repeats itself," the old woman thought and whispered. "Let's hope it's not for the worse…"

And she crossed herself once more, turned and without looking back again quickly made off to the village.

Belinko's former wife had learnt everything. The fishermen's wives passed regularly through her house and spoke in detail about the beauty of the new woman, and the large hut in the forest…. The women would talk as if randomly, but from time to time they'd dart sideways looks at the former wife's face.

"And he still hasn't come to see you?" they'd ask just like that, as if by-the-way.

The former wife would shake her head and turn whiter still.

"Ey, I'll be going…" the guest would stand up and add reassuringly. "There, don't you worry, he'll surely come, but you know don't you… He's now got a young pretty woman, he has to pay her more attention… I'm sure that later he'll find time to call on you…"

The former wife would nod and close the door behind her, now with her face turning green.

CHAOS

Much time passed before Belinko crossed the threshold of the little house, in which he'd grown up.

All the village noticed his coming, they held their breaths and sharpened their ears. They only heard indistinct voices from inside and long explanations, muffled shouts, the familiar crash of breakages and two juicy slaps in the end.

After that Belinko dispatched his first wife somewhere, demolished Granny Dushka's old house, divided the big garden in two, cut down the trees around it, widened it, dug and began to build. He dug out foundations in one of the gardens... He dug out foundations in the other as well.

At this time the village children visited the second wife in the forest. They gathered in a circle around her and looked at her in silence. She was not fazed by their searching looks, she smiled at them, and imbued them with tenderness. She was a woman who loved children. A woman who wanted to have children. She talked to them, as if in a story, about the world from which she came, it opened up before their eyes and no longer seemed so unknown and scary. They listened with gaping mouths and they saw wonderful pictures.

"And have you heard of Atlantis?" asked Mavri's youngest son.

His big brother was far away from him and couldn't whack him on the back of his head.

The woman smile grew wider, then she became serious and nodded.

"Tell us," another child begged.

She opened her mouth, but before she could utter a word, Mavri's second son ran up and his shouts made them rush to the cliff edge.

Something new had appeared.

15

It was neither a pirate ship nor a huge sea monster.

An old peeling boat was approaching their shore and was deftly avoiding the reefs. The man on board clearly knew the sea here like the back of his hand, like the local fishermen.

The children rushed down the path, lined up on the small port and waited.

They did not see that Granny Vanda had left her knitting and was standing in front of her house, almost hanging out over the sea, looking with the same curiosity towards the newcomer. But, in contrast to the children, she recognized this boat and knew who could be aboard it.

At the quay a man with white hair leapt up, unexpectedly agile for his years,. He tied up the boat, away from the others and took the upward path, without noticing the crowd of children.

The boys looked at one another and quickly set out after him. Their curiosity flared up even more, because it was clear he was making for the abandoned house up on the clifftop.

The man walked with the same huge rolling stride their fathers had, like a man who'd spent his life on the sea. He passed Granny Vanda, looked at her and stopped. He hesitated then entered her yard and stood before the old woman. She'd returned under the walnut tree and was sitting on her chair. The stranger bent down, took her wrinkled hand in his huge hands, held it and then kissed it. He remained a little longer without saying anything, then he turned and left.

The boys watched in astonishment.

CHAOS

Granny Vanda continued to hold the unravelled black cardigan, but the needles lay abandoned on her knees. And thinking over the last little hour of what had just happened, she looked out after the man with eyes turned inward on her memories.

He climbed the cliff and reached the edge. He took a deep breath, his eyes touched the sea, and only then he slowly relaxed and stopped at the house. He approached it somewhat cautiously, stretched out a hand and touched the walls, as if to caress them. The plaster fell away beneath his fingers. He gave the old beams a friendly tap, feeling their strength over the time, he walked round the building several times, stood in front of the door and froze.

The boys froze along with him, and even without that they'd held their breath throughout all this ritual.

He took a string from his neck with an old rusty key.

The children's noses itched even more with curiosity, they emerged from their astonishment, crowded behind his back and from there peered with large rounded eyes.

The man put the key into the lock, turned it and opened up. The door gave a long drawn out screech. Cobwebs festooned the interior, the smell wafted of stale abandonment, of mould and secrecy. The boys craned their necks. He didn't see them, didn't feel them behind his back. His thoughts were racing somewhere back to the time, he was living in those other years and all his senses only accepted what had been back then. He walked inside and without turning, he closed the door in front of their dumbstruck open mouths. In a while his voice was heard, quiet and tender, talking of someone. And it seemed to the children that they heard another voice as well, which answered him with the same tenderness. They stayed by the door and listened, then they began to circle round and try to peer inside. But the windows were covered in a thick curtain of dust, gathered over years and this stopped them seeing what the man was doing there.

The sun was setting. The boys sat again on the cliff, but now with their backs to the sea. Their eyes did not leave windows and door of the house.

"What's the Sailor doing inside?" Mavri's second son asked and thus gave a name to the stranger.

A low ray of the sun alighted on the dusty glass and it seemed to them that they saw how within the house a woman was walking by the windows, draped in a short coat. She stopped before the clear outline of the sailor, sitting on a chair, stroked his head and held him to her breasts... The ray disappeared and the vision was gone. From the sea a light breeze blew up which gave them goose-pimples.

A little lower down, Granny Vanda was sitting under the walnut, still with her arms hanging loose, and she didn't think of finishing off the last stitches on her black cardigan. Her knitting was at an end - that meant autumn was now on its way. And the old woman listened to the lonesome tolling of the bell. Who was departing?

The next day Mavri had to thrash the tree.

16

Now Granddad Nacho was no more.
The line of old folk on the low stone was gradually thinning out. He'd departed quietly and suddenly. In the evening his pub was working, he closed it as always but the next afternoon he simply didn't turn up. On the next day the verger rang the bell for him. The son and daughter-in-law closed the pub, hurried to clean and throw out his stuff, and when later the bell rang for Granny Visha, they gathered the household items, locked the door and left for the big city.

The bell fell silent again. The old folk would sit beneath it every afternoon, shrunken, their hair turning white. With tightened hearts they looked upwards. When would it ring for them?

The verger had been avoiding them for a long time. He rolled his cigarettes on his own at the bottom of the yard with his yellowing wrinkled fingers and didn't dare look at them. He'd disappear for long periods, no-one knew where.

One day, out of the little room at the bottom of the bell tower, two strange men carried out someone for whom the bell did not ring. It was the old verger. In the wake of his ordinary wooden coffin there was only one mourner, Homeless Petra.

17

The house on top of the cliff stood closed and lonely. There was no sign that anyone was living inside. During the day no window or door was opened. And after dusk fell it remained as dark and silent as before.

The children gathered every morning, circled the silent walls, glued their ears to the door and it seemed to them that they heard voices within which whispered quietly and tenderly. The boys would look at each other, circle again, try to peep through some crack, but the windows remained covered in dust like fully drawn curtains, and gave no access to a stranger's eye.

The kids would sit with their backs to the sea. They fixed their eyes on the door and waited.

The Sailor did not come out.

Now that the old verger was gone, Petra became even more lonely. She had no-one to share her food with, to sit with, and simply not talk. And know that someone was thinking about her, and cared, like she too thought about him. Then with some unknown sense she sniffed out the unknown solitary presence high up over the sea. Before midday she began to visit all the barns, gathered up the food left for her, and carried it up the path. She climbed to the clifftop house, sat on the threshold, set out the food on a cloth, ate a little, wrapped up the rest and left it. She knocked on the door, and drew back down the path. After a while the door creaked open, with the same drawn out squeak, a hand stretched out from inside, took the bundle, and withdrew.

CHAOS

The children narrowed their eyes but couldn't see anything. When Petra turned up they'd draw back so as not to get in her way. They'd wait for her to eat in peace and then leave before again circling the house.

In the afternoon the door would open and the hand would leave the cloth, carefully folded in the same place.

At dusk, Homeless Petra would come up the path and sit on the doorstep, put the cloth over her knees, lean her back on the door and fix her eyes on the sea.

The boys would pull back again and leave her alone, without taking their excited eyes off her.

Petra would sit silent, self-absorbed, her face would relax, and from time to time a quick smile would flit across it. Then she'd sigh, stand up and set out again down towards the night, which awaited her in some barn.

The boys would follow her and quiet sighs would escape from their small chests. In front of their eyes, the siren from the bay would be swimming again, with the sparkling drops on her pale skin and golden hair. They'd get up and follow her as if spellbound. And they believed that story the sirens were born from sea foam and they'd turn back into foam.

Then Homeless Petra stopped coming. Teo, the youngest Krayan and the only one of his family left, had married her to the surprize of the whole village, and now she wouldn't leave his house. The boys suddenly felt as if they'd been robbed and for the first time in their childish brains, they felt jealousy.

18

Teo set out to find Homeless Petra. He got up early in the morning and went round the village looking into barn after barn, he saw scattered blankets, food remains, but there was no sign of Petra. He went to the sea shore, he stepped over the shingle, climbed the rocks but didn't see her anywhere.

He passed by the church, nodded to the silent old folk, peered into the verger's gaping abandoned little room under the bell tower.

At dusk he returned, tired with weakened legs. It crossed his mind that he could easily find her at night, curled up in some barn, but he didn't want to disturb her sleep. And he himself could not sleep, the loneliness of the big house chased away the peace and quiet of the night, it squeezed and gnawed at his soul. All his life up till now repeated itself before his eyes. Teo saw his Grandfather Krayan's last hours, saved in his childish memories. He again lived through the final sad days of his grandmother, he felt the touch of her bony cold hand, heard her quiet whisper. "Marry Homeless Petra... No-one should stay alone." The flies circled the little room, and one of them was crawling on the tongue of the gaping mouth. With this memory, Teo curled up into a ball as if to protect himself from something and wept unstoppable childish tears. He wanted to tell someone, to pour out all his grief, but there was no-one. "If they tell you that cold hands mean a warm heart, they're lying to you dearie... A stove can't burn and its pipes be cold..." What were Homeless Petra's hands like? When he found her the first thing he had to do was touch her hands....

CHAOS

As he went round the village and hunted out signs of Homeless Petra, Teo unconsciously set off up the path to the cliff top. He passed by Granny Vanda's house and saw the old woman put on her black cardigan. Teo hesitated for just a moment, pushed open the gate and entered before Granny Vanda had picked up her chair and gone back indoors. He ran up to her and grabbed her arm. The old woman looked into his eyes and understood everything. She sat back on her chair and signalled to him to sit on the ground next to her. Teo folded his legs and, staring ahead at the sea, began to talk. He poured out everything which had been crushing his spirits for so long, sharing his pain and fear of loneliness. In the end, blushing and with head held down, he spoke of his Granny's wish that he should marry Homeless Petra, and that this wish was his as well. And with time it had become ever stronger.

With these words, Granny Vanda shivered at the strength of his desire for a woman who not only belonged to everyone, but brought destruction with her ravaged soul. She was all over goose pimples, because she realized that nothing could stop him, that he himself was ready to destroy everything which stood in his path to homeless Petra. And when she took breath, the old woman tried to help him, before the dark forces overcame his reason entirely.

"Go back down the path and wait for her," said Granny Vanda and stood up. "She'll pass by soon..."

She took the chair and set off for the house. Before entering, she looked after Teo, who was now running down the path, and muttered as his shape hurried towards its fate, "And God help you, even though He's helpless before the devil...."

She crossed herself and went indoors, to only emerge after the winter, knowing that she could not prevent the inevitable. She just prayed for it not to be as bad as she saw it.

LYUDMILA ANDROVSKA

Teo took his stand at the beginning of the path, relieved at unloading the weight of his pain and memories on to someone else and now impatient in expectation.

Petra appeared, dressed as always in her strange frayed clothes, with the bundle of food in her hand. And with the premonition for something unusual, something different from every other time, which would turn her life upside down. She was not surprized when suddenly the youth stepped in front of her, took her hand and spoke to her. She was sure that he'd never stood in a queue for her, that he neither knew about nor even suspected such a queue... She looked at him with her big bright eyes, as though listening to some voice within herself, and gave no answer. She continued up the path, left the food on the threshold, knocked on the door and when the Sailor took the bundle, Homeless Petra did not leave as usual. She remained there, leaning her back against the wall and looking out into the sea. She stayed there the whole afternoon, all the way to evening, and when the Sailor returned the cloth, she straightened up and set off back.

Down at the beginning of the path, Teo was waiting for her, fingers burning for the touch of her hands.

When she entered the big Krayan house, Petra did not believe her luck. To be conducted into the only two story house was the dream of every girl in the village, so how had Teo fancied and chosen her exactly? And as if in a dream she stepped over the white threshold with fear and respect.

But her fear disappeared no later than the first days, Petra came to believe she was not dreaming and love began to emerge from within her. Love towards the home. Her home. It hid her from the surrounding world, protected her from cold and evil looks, it warmed her and enfolded her. Behind its thick strong walls Homeless Petra at last felt security. Behind its firmly bolted door she felt protected. This was a home that cared about her. And for which she would care, with tenderness, love and utter devotion. Her first and only home. And

CHAOS

Petra relaxed into the home's embrace and at last fell into a really deep healthy sleep. She slept long, slept for an entire month, she had to sleep out so many years. But before sinking into the sleep oblivion, she realised, still half awake, that she hadn't married Teo, she'd married his house.

A home gave protection. A home gave security. And not only that. It gave warmth, comfort, beauty and harmony. It fed and preserved love for longer. It gave a feeling of mutuality.

Belinko had realized this for a long time. Over the years of wandering from place to place, to wherever the chaos inside him drove him, he thought ever more frequently about Granny Dushka's little warm house. And he knew that one day he would return.

And now he was building. He was building a home. And not just one. Row by row the two houses were built up in their two gardens, which he'd walled round. One next to the other, identical, with enormous bright windows, slowly they crept up from the ground towards the branches of the trees. Two houses for his two wives. Now separated from his first wife, he had suddenly realized that he did not want to lose her forever. Then Belinko had never lived with her at all, had not enjoyed her, had not been sated with her caresses and presence. She had to be close by, very close to him, so he didn't take his eyes off her. And not allow anyone else to grab her. He built the houses so that each garden was visible to the other...

When Granny Vanda put on her new black cardigan, and retired to her house, the first floor of the two houses was ready.

Mavri thrashed the tree in his mother's garden and carried off a great pile of walnuts to his house.

Having knitted the new village events with the last stitches into the black cardigan, Granny Vanda sat in her cottage, looked through the small window at the sea and her thoughts ranged indiscriminately over time – the past, present and future. There was so much to think over, to guess how things would develop ahead. As she thought of

Teo, and old Krayanka's last words, the old woman shivered. How had Krayanka wanted to bring a person into her home who had never had anything? Hadn't she thought that someone who had lived in deprivation, becomes voracious when they come to possession? And the thirst of selfishness would drive them to grab even more for themselves alone, even when they need no more. As if someone who's spent a long time in the desert finds themselves standing on the shore of a huge lake – it's not enough to drink the water, but to throw themselves in and want to swallow it all with all the pores of their body. Petra was just such a dried out thirsty person; Teo's Granny had just brought her to the lake, and dipped her in it, let's hope the Homeless won't swallow it all.

"God give Teo luck," the old woman muttered to herself, but she lost belief, as she thought about Petra's father and the chaos of his destructive cells.

The old woman looked out. As with every autumn at this time, cold rains began to fall.

The men walked round the bare walls of both of Belinko's houses, soaked through.

"Shame!" they tutted. "It gives no cover..."

Belinko didn't look worried, he had something else in mind.

He stood under the rain, as if fused to the cliff. The sailor carefully observed the sea. For the first time he'd appeared outside his house, since his arrival. He looked at the sea, as if he was seeking something in it, and from blue and calm, it had gradually become green and savage, then black and terrifying. Tall black waves reared up and hit the rocks with a malevolent gurgling. The roar of the vast dark water strengthened. Hanging over the abyss, the Sailor stood motionless and waited. And when the storm spoke with its full force, he walked down the path, untied the boat from its dock, took the oars and lost himself amid the huge waves.

CHAOS

Granny Vanda saw him from the window and made the sign of the cross behind him. Maybe only she knew.

Teo saw him as well. He was standing close to the harbour, there where for the first time he'd met and stopped Petra, he'd submitted his burning forehead to the rain and wind. Swallowed up in his worrying thoughts he barely recognized the stranger and paid him no attention.

Teo had worries. For near on a month Petra was sleeping. He made her food, took it to the bed, woke her up just to feed her, just like he'd fed his Granny, in her last days, and then left her to drift again into sleep. He'd glue his ear to her breasts, reassuring himself that she was breathing, but nothing was capable of waking her up. Teo was even pleased. He didn't know how to behave to her when she awoke, what to do, what to say to her.

And when in the morning Petra stretched out in the bed, looked around in surprize and got up, he dropped his head in embarrassment. He'd lain next to her and made love to her in her sleep. He felt as though he'd been caught in a crime scene.

"Oh I'm hungry" she exclaimed as she stretched again and licked her lips sweetly.

Relieved, Teo rushed to the kitchen and in a second ran back with a saucepan from which wafted an aromatic steam. Petra impatiently thrust out her hands and their fingers touched. Teo pulled back as if scalded by their heat and almost spilled the soup. He turned red and jumped from foot to foot. Petra burst out laughing, looked at him flirtatiously and began to slurp greedily. And Teo jumped outside and hurried to find work beneath the rain. He didn't come inside the whole day. This was welcomed by her, she got up and set to walking from room to room, to get to know the house, she went everywhere, opened all the doors, peered into every corner of both floors. And she felt mistress of this castle...

19

Petra liked one room. She set to cleaning, washing, tidying up, from somewhere she took out a roll of home-woven cloth and put up curtains. She called Teo. He ran in wet and bristling. And trembling but not from cold.

"This will be our room," she said laughing.

He nodded, happy and dropped his head. He was pleased she'd thought of him as well, that she'd thought of the pair of them... and he was impressed at how quickly she'd orientated herself and taken things into her own hands.

Petra looked at him carefully and tried to tell from his face whether he was pleased. She felt grateful to him, hadn't he brought her here and allowed her to feel the mistress. For her Teo was inextricably linked to the house. Her home and he were one whole, which was hers alone. She had to take care of them. Everything depended on her... And she looked at him with tenderness. She saw his confused look, his body shaking from soaking cold water. Her eyes warmed, she stretched out her slender fingers and slowly and carefully began to unstick his wet clothes from his goose-pimpled skin. Teo trembled even more from their heat and he twisted under her caresses. Petra laughed, her eyes sparkled with fire, she pressed her whole body him to him, and with one hand pulled off the counterpane which just a little earlier she'd spread over the wide wooden bed. She also swept back the heavy covers and stretched out over the white thick sheet. She pulled Teo towards her, he quickly popped into the bed and curled up on the edge, far from her. Petra again took matters into her gentle hands, sought him with

CHAOS

her hot palms and drew him in. Quite faint, Teo cuddled into her and pressed his sweaty cheek into her breasts. And then he sensed that long forgotten smell of warmth and goodness, a smell of security and safety. The smell of a mother's embrace. The woman next to him was stroking him like a little child and was kissing the hairs on his head that were sticking up from tension.

On that first night, Homeless Petra opened up another world for Teo, a new life, that looked like a chasm into which he was falling, swimming, bumping into feelings not experienced till now, he was rocked by sweet pains and faintness and painful tremors coursed through his body. In this vast time in which days and nights merged into one, the hot ball in his chest, gathered heat and erupted like a volcano. A calming warmth poured out into his loins, his hands, even as far as his toes.

For Teo life stopped existing, everything turned back into night, into endless night, sunk into the smouldering body of Homeless Petra and her scalding soul.

Outside cold rain poured down, which turned gradually into snow.

20

The trees in the forest around the village froze with ice welded to their branches and hanging in crystal shards.

In these cold days the fishermen, did not come out, they huddled in the warmth of their houses and gnawed at salt fish.

Only the shouts from Belinko's hut seeped out into the surrounding silence. His second wife was giving birth. Belinko paced clumsily around her and wondered whether to hold back his hand or to squeeze her big heaving tummy. Everything began so unexpectedly quickly, that he hadn't even been able to call Granny Vanda, and now he worried about leaving his wife alone.

Close to the hut, hidden between the ice-laden trees, Mavri hungrily drank in every shriek, pressing the cold sharpness of his axe to his face.

Mavri liked to listen, when babies were born. Even as a young boy he'd accompany his mother and with no-one noticing him in the chaos, he'd crane to see what was happening with his ears pricked up. He experienced an inexplicable attraction to the secrets of new life emerging. He liked to see his wife with a growing belly, and with the birth of every one of his sons, Granny Vanda was unable to chase him out of the room. Mavri would busy himself about her, supposedly to help but only got in the way. When she managed to chase him outside the door, he'd put his ear to the keyhole, and his whole body turned into a receiver. His wife's cries as she gave birth calmed the tumult within him and spread peace to his soul.

CHAOS

Tight to the trees, Mavri now caught every cry from the hut and his imagination painted the scene inside. The snowflakes stuck to him and melted immediately.

Footsteps were heard and Mavri made himself small. His mother, Granny Vanda was walking through the forest. The old woman knew that Belinko's second wife would soon need her help and she'd come herself to check whether the time had come.

Mavri waited for her to enter the hut and then quickly distanced himself. His shape sank into the trees and falling snow. He charged out of the forest, then he circled the village and made his way to the shore. A blessed tranquillity poured through his entire body.

By the sea under the falling snowflakes, he found peace. Mavri noticed his sons and the other lads by the harbour. He knew that the children often went there to look out for the Sailor's boat.

The fishermen were circling too. Just like that, as though by chance, but they exchanged hidden looks and sighed.

The storm had died down. And the Sailor returned. He tied his boat up in the usual place and slowly made his way under the inquisitive stares of the children and adults. He paid them no attention, he didn't even notice them, he shut himself inside the house, bolted the door and after a while smoke appeared from the chimney.

The men realized that nothing more was going to happen and they left. The children climbed the cliff, took what food they'd secretly taken from home, out of the wide pockets of their winter clothes, lined it up in front of the door and knocked. They pulled back to one side and waited. After a while the door creaked, and the Sailor's hand appeared from inside, gathered the food and took it in. The bolt went home. Satisfied, the children left. Petra could no longer care for the solitary man, and they had wordlessly agreed to stand in for her.

They descended down the path and made their way into the village to hunt for mice. They often saw some cat, staying motionless and concentrated before a crack in the wall, or running across the white snow with a brownish body between its teeth and a long mousy tail hanging from its mouth. This happened ever more rarely, were the mice dying out or were they hiding from the cold deep in their holes?

Quiet and calm covered the village along with the smoke hanging over it. And smoke came from the Sailor's cottage. There was smoke too from Belinko's hut.

Belinko did not show his nose outside, he huddled by the hot fire and by the even hotter body of his young bright-eyed wife, playing with his first baby and making a second one.

Somewhere in the vicinity, Mavri passed by occasionally. The snow outside held them back.

21

The whole winter Teo wandered round the house in a daze. Petra pulled back a curtain in front of his eyes, and behind it he discovered something new and unfamiliar, which gave him no peace. It forced him to continuously seek her body, her caresses, the touch of her warm skin. When Petra got fed up and pushed him away, he'd curl up in some corner, and follow her with wide open crazy eyes. She wondered what to do and found him jobs outside, as far away as possible. Usually she'd send him to the forest for wood.

Teo would rush off, quickly chop off branches, and run back on the double.

The days passed without him noticing them, they left no memory, in the quivering anticipation of the new dive into the hot abyss, sunk into the memory of the previous thrill.

And there, at the bottom, amidst the dizzying waves of the chaos that overwhelmed him, everything within him was screaming from love.

22

The winter was over.

Belinko continued to build – a row of bricks for one house, a row of bricks for the other. He'd laid the ceiling over the ground floor and begun to build the second story. And again it was one row of bricks in one house, then one row of bricks in the other.

The fishermen came round and tut-tutted. "It'll collapse, Belinko, man," they said, "How will you build another flor when there's no earth below to support it?"

Belinko paid no heed and smiled, "And Krayan's house?"

"The Krayans," the people waved their hands. "They're something else... They were capable."

Of course they had old Krayan in mind – who built the big house.

"They're no different," Belinko answered. "If they can build a two story house, so can I..."

And he lined up brick after brick. He laid them in one house, then come down, run to the other yard, climb to the second floor and start laying there.

There was nothing left for the men but to get down to helping him. They'd lain about too long during the winter and they wanted to stretch their muscles. They were happy to get stuck in. Belinko watched what they were doing, gave advice, threw out some joke. And he looked proudly over to his wife and his little boy, who were standing close by.

Towards the end of spring, they topped off one house and Belinko immediately installed his second wife with the child.

Then he topped off the second. His first wife returned.

CHAOS

The village women began to circle round and peer into both yards. They sharpened their ears and waited to hear any quarrelling between Belliku's two wives. They were certain that sooner or later something would happen.

After building the houses, the fishermen dispersed and began looking out to sea, but they didn't get into their boats. They were waiting for a sign. Granny Vanda's signal.

And when at last she brought her chair out under the walnut and took off her black cardigan, they knew their time had come. They turned their eyes to the cliff to see if the Sailor would appear. But he did not emerge. People didn't know what to think until Granny Vanda told them the story at the same time as she unravelled the cardigan, reading it from the loops… Here in the black stitches, she'd knitted everything that had happened in the village for years till now. Perhaps a little differently, seen through her viewpoint and fragmented in her eyes. Perhaps not quite as it had happened… Perhaps the story which it told was just in her thoughts… Maybe the man in the cottage was not the same. But let Granny Vanda tell the story and everyone crowded around her and listened…

23

"Many years ago, a fisherman lived in this house with his wife and young son. The boy grew up, began to go out fishing in the sea with his father and year after year became a young man. One after the other the parents departed on their final journey and left him alone along with the house on the cliff and the boat, tied up at the quay. He disappeared and for many years no-one heard anything about him, until the rumour reached the village that he was a sailor on a trawler. His house was abandoned and the boat rotted in the harbour water.

"One day he returned, now married and bringing a wife with him. She was young and beautiful, the fishermen had never seen such beauty till now. Her face was like the foam on the waves, her hair was reddening like the sunset and her eyes as changeable as the sea.

"As beautiful as Homeless Petra!" one of the lads cried out and everyone looked at him, amazed. He hunched up under their reproachful looks and along with all the other lads he blushed.

"The fisherman's son brought her to the house, they stayed a few days, then he was off sailing again. She stayed up there on her own. In a short time the house changed – from a grey thing merging into the cliff, it suddenly it straightened and brightened up, curtains and flowers warmed the windows. The husband returned ever more frequently, running up the path with big impatient strides and when leaving he'd walk slowly with his head hung low.

"Sometimes the sailor's wife came down to the village, picked up this and that, and then returned up there again.

CHAOS

When a storm blew up, the wife stood on the cliff and didn't return indoors until the sea calmed down. In the village it was whispered that she cast spells to keep her husband safe. And this was repeated with his every departure and every storm.

Once he'd left again, and in a few days' time, a hurricane blew up the like of which even the oldest could not remember. And their memories went way back, so many years, as old as themselves.

The wife went out on the cliff, and wrapped in an old winter coat, she fixed her eyes on the huge black waves. Her lips silently whispered something. Darkness engulfed her but no-one was surprized. The next day as early as dawn they saw her, continuing to stand and look out to the savage sea, almost merging with the dark grey sky. She sat and whispered her prayers to the storm to protect her husband. Darkness fell again and she huddled in her coat and waited...

On the third morning, the storm continued, but she wasn't there. The Fishermen were surprized, they looked up there the whole day, and when she did not appear in the evening, they entered the house to look for her. Inside there was no-one, two small rooms gaped empty. Then some of them suggested that the high waves had swept her away during the night. Or someone else said she'd fallen on her own into the sea.

The hurricane died down and they went to find the sailor's wife on the shore. If only the sea would at least wash up her body, people thought and for days on end they circled the cliffs nearby, but they found nothing. In time they only found her old coat, which she'd thrown away.

After a month her husband returned. He climbed to the house at the double, and the fishermen stood at the foot of the path and watched him in silence. Only when he emerged, not believing his own eyes, they climbed up and told him. He stood and listened, not a muscle twitching on his face. He stayed silent a long time and in the end he uttered something.

Only those who were closest to him heard.

"The sea takes those it loves," he stretched out his hand, took the coat, pressed it to his body and added "And it sends a sign that it won't give them back."

He turned and began to climb the path to the house, his figure shrank, pressed by the grey sky.

In the following days they saw him at the harbour, pulling up the boat on to the shore, fixing and caulking it. Then both he and the boat disappeared. No-one saw him again. That was a long, long time ago.

As they listened the boys remembered the woman they'd spotted through the dusty windows. A young woman, wrapped in an old coat...

And the children quivered from eternity's touch.

24

Her life with Teo opened up something new for Homeless Petra, something unfamiliar to her till now – her being with one man only, hers alone, every day and every night. And when she felt only one painfully familiar body, Petra would reach her hands back and dig them into the hard wall. Her nails gouged deep grooves into the mortar and bloody smears were left over it, she'd bite her fingers and suck them over again... Taste of whitewash, brick, strong walls. Taste of security.

The house gave her this security as well. And Petra would stretch out her hands towards the wall and make more and more gouges in it, getting ever deeper. The blood from her wounded fingers soaked deep into the plaster and lime and sand accumulated in her wounds.

And when Teo succumbed to the whirlwind of his new feelings, Petra caressed the walls around her bed with her legs, with her whole body, giving in to them.

Every night Homeless Petra made love to the house.

Somewhere very far back were left the nights in the straw, the clumsy furtive steps by the barns and the unfamiliar male bodies, which squeezed her with hoarse gasping and the lustful smell of sweat. But her home, her present home, the only one she had, had not just raised its walls between her and all the rest of the world. It cut her life decisively and definitively into two. It had cut her off forever from the past. And Petra repaid it with her love.

She didn't understand at what moment exactly she began to separate Teo from her love for the house. Teo and his house were two different things, and day by day she separated them further away from each other. The gouges in the mortar became deep, red with blood, as if it flowed and beat through the whole house. And Petra's fingers whitened and became as hard as the plaster that encrusted them and drank in their warmth.

The love that Petra felt towards her home, burnt in Mavri as well. The same love drove him to continually seek out the desired body of his wife, then to see it swell up again, filled with future life.

For a long time now his wife didn't let him near her, she'd silently set out his supper and go to the other room, where their five sons would stand between them like an unbreakable barrier of bristling cockerels. They'd now grown up, Mavri looked them over, they were five little men, who jealously guarded their mother, from the other, from the big man.

At the time when he saw his children opposing him, Mavri would turn and slam the door behind him. He'd wander round the barns in the village, find Homeless Petra and seek release in her compliant body. He didn't know that with Petra he had a common father. He didn't know that this father in his youth had also sought release from the chaos within himself in the body of his little sister. He did not know that he was turning in an endless circle, going back to the beginning and closing the wheel.

Now Mavri was silent before the bristling looks of his sons. He'd turn and slam the door, go outside and set out round the village. He'd pass several times by Belinko's house and his eyes would devour the ever broadening figure of Belinko's wife. Those cries again ran through his ears, those he'd heard in the wintry forest, when unconsciously he'd lifted his axe to his face, for the shiny metal to cool the chaos raging inside him.

Through the windows in the neighbouring house he carefully watched Belinko's first wife.

Belinko's life with the beautiful woman that he'd got one child with and was expecting another from, dug a poisoned chisel into her

CHAOS

soul and sowed dark desires within her. But wife number one knew how to suppress them, she'd noticed that Belinko's attraction to her was not over. She kept watch for him to be on his own in the yard, she'd come out to, she'd smile, and as if no longer interested in him she would undertake some task. As she realized that he was furtively observing her, she found a reason to lift her skirts a little, as though they were hindering her movements, and to undo the top buttons of her blouse, because she suddenly felt hot. She'd stop for two or three seconds to give him the chance to look her over, then she'd turn and walk gracefully back inside. Belinko was left in the yard with mouth wide open.

By now the village men were secretly observing both women, and waiting for something to happen with bated breath. Outwardly nothing happened.

The fishermen turned their attention to the cats. There were no mice, they'd disappeared, like some miracle and the men began a fight with the scrawny cats, cats which were no longer quite so scrawny. They put out poison, set traps, they aimed flintlocks, chased them with axes, but didn't manage to kill even one. The cats hid in the yard of Belinko's second wife.

25

Early in the morning the Sailor took his stand at the top of the cliff. The fishermen were just getting ready to go out to sea, when they saw him. A vague premonition stopped them. They turned their eyes to the walnut tree – Granny Vanda was not here. The men moored their boats and went home. From time to time they peered out through their windows and looked towards the cliff. And every time they saw the Sailor's fixed shape.

Towards midday he sea suddenly darkened, a strong wind blew up and a powerful storm came out of nowhere.

Only Granny Vanda saw how the Sailor descended past her house, untied his boat from the quay and disappeared into the waves. Her hand simply rose to her forehead and she made the sign of the cross. Then she made a cross over him.

The storm was over just as quickly as it had begun. In a few hours the wind blew the clouds away and the sky brightened. The waves decreased and by sunset the sea glinted smooth as a mirror.

The children ran to the cliff. After them both the men and women emerged. Granny Vanda too stood outside her house.

Everyone was waiting. The yell from one of Mavri's children alerted them, he was pointing at something out to sea. People's necks craned, eyes strained and the saw a small dot which was approaching their shore.

Relieved sighs burst from their lungs.

26

Homeless Petra dedicated herself to her home. She dedicated herself with everything she had. With her time, with her worries, with her love. Teo would be continuously behind her. His following her with servile loving eyes irritated her.

If she went out into the yard, he'd come out after her. Petra would finish her work under his unwavering stare and nervously make back for the house, with the secret hope that he wouldn't follow her. Before going inside she'd stop on the threshold and diligently clean her slippers. Only then would she step inside. She carried this out so punctiliously that it resembled a sacred ritual.

Teo would set out after her, distracted by the sight of her. Then he'd enter. Petra would be aware of him, with back turned looking out to see if he stopped on the doormat, or stepped as she expected on to the floor tiles sparkling with cleanliness, so she'd chase him outside, with her shouts. She'd stand in the doorway, bright red and puffing in indignation, she made sure that he wouldn't be coming in again and immediately set down again to polishing the place where he'd left traces of his footprints.

Teo got in her way. His presence did not allow her to experience the house during the day with all her senses, to hear its noises and to immerse herself in its smell. To be alone beside its walls. And she always found a reason to chase him away, to receive him late at night in the dark and within his embrace feel the cuddle of the house.

27

When a second child appeared the rumour crept through the village that Belinko had begun popping over to the neighbouring house, to his first wife.

The men lost sleep, they tossed and turned all through the night, came out into their yards and in the meagre moonlight tried to see the figure running between the two houses. Sometimes they thought they made out a lurking dark shadow, but they weren't sure.

During the say they found work close to the house of Belinko's second wife and waited for her to notice them. Dark male desires, unknown to them till now, had awakened in them. Is such a beautiful woman to be abandoned? The men sighed and wondered at Belinko's sanity.

The women also happily circled around. Their suspicions were justified, their premonitions were aroused. They looked for some change, they hoped to spot dark shadows beneath her eyes or giveaway sunken wrinkles from accumulated bitterness. Their predatory looks fixed on the face of Belinko's second wife and felt it out centimetre by centimetre, piercing every pore. But she stayed the same, her two confinements had not altered her fluid body, her fluffy hair shone around her smiling face. And she was forever singing and chatting.

The children crept behind her and played with the unhappy persecuted cats who found shelter here and a caress. She fed them, stroked them and they trustingly curled themselves round her feet and purred happily. Their smooth hair shone in the sun like her hair and like the golden braids of Homeless Petra...

28

Now that she'd become a married woman and mistress of a large house, Homeless Petra began to pleat her hair into two thick braids, which hung over her shoulders and breasts. In the evening she'd untie them, sitting on the bed, with her back pressed to the wall, so she continually feel the touch of the house.

Teo would love to watch her. Her fingers would slowly creep down one braid first, the freed hair lapped about her neck, her shoulders, hid them, and a little further down her erect nipples would peep out shyly.

Teo would go to her and stretch out his hands, he'd touch her hair so cautiously as if he was scared it would fall apart in his fingers, then he'd bury his face into its scent. Petra would freeze, her skin would bristle and her hair divide into separate electrified threads. Teo could not hold out, he'd grab her and squash her beneath him, and she would stretch her hands back and sink them into the wall, in deep furrows.

Love welled up in Teo, it tormented him, gnawed at him, pressed his innards. Apart from the short night-time moments, Petra gave him nothing else and his love sought a release, over which he'd could continually erupt. Teo understood that his body was too small to accommodate her and rejected by her strength, could find no place.

He heard Petra's angry shout from the house, and immediately after that her hand appeared at the door and threw out a little grey hairy ball.

Teo stared inquisitively, hesitated, circled, and stepped tentatively towards the motionless bundle. The kitten lay on the grass as it had fallen. As if it was wondering what to do now, without paying attention to the surrounding world.

LYUDMILA ANDROVSKA

Teo stretched out a hand and touched it cautiously, stroked its matted fur, wiped its eyes and tipped its little pink nose. Without moving the kitten trustingly licked his finger. He picked it up and it lost itself in his big hands, unkempt and helpless.

From this day on, Teo dedicated to it all the care and tenderness which he wanted to bestow on Petra, but which she rejected with such tenacity and perseverance. He fed it, stroked it, played with it. The kitten repaid him only with its love.

Why do they say that cats don't love humans and only connect with the home?

29

Belinko was confused. And this confusion sowed additional frustration into the chaos he bore within him.

Before his eyes there would continually appear the woman who was once his, but for a long time now had set up her life without him. And she didn't hide the fact that there was no place for Belinko with her. He would have imagined matters somewhat differently when he built the two houses and wanted her to be in his line of vision.

His second wife dedicated all her time to the two children, busied herself with the cats, and ever more rarely thought about him. Whenever she relaxed in his arms for a moment, in the short moments of rest, something always cropped up to interrupt them. Belinko didn't notice whether what had frustrated them was a child or a cat, He'd jump up in agitation, go out into the yard and look out at the windows of the neighbouring house.

His first wife would see him, hidden in the darkness of the windows and the next day would find a way of stirring up the chaos in his soul even more.

The grey cats loved the home that sheltered and protected them from the hatred of the village. They walked through the yard, with a joyful confidence, but just in case looked to keep further away from Belinko. He hadn't done anything bad to them, but they distrusted him with their feline instinct.

They ran away in fright and they all huddled together like a big ash-grey ball at the feet of Belinko's second wife, when in the middle of the day for the whole village to see him, Belinko went to his first wife's house.

He pottered in the yard, did this and that like a homeowner and sat under the vine to drink rakia, accompanied by a salad that his first wife brought out. Then he entered the house. His first wife collected the glass and the plate and followed him with submissive steps.

The village held its breath and waited behind their windows for Belinko to emerge.

On the next morning Belinko's wife appeared. She was carrying a big pile of clothes and she threw them over the fence into the neighbouring yard. She went back, took the shoes with the heels cut off, which Belinko wore in the house, threw them on the pile and cleaned out all traces of him. After that she took on all the obvious masculine work that he'd been doing up till then.

No-one appeared from the other house.

Only when the second wife fed the cats and brought the children home for lunch, did the door furtively open and the first wife ran out. Not a trace of her victorious look from the previous day remained. She grabbed the clothes and shoes and carried them through the yard. One trouser leg dragged sadly along the ground behind her and tried to catch on to something.

From the other yard the grey cats watched her with narrowed eyes. The village stayed silent and watched.

30

Petra rarely came out into the yard.

The disgusting little creature who had invaded her realm and whom she had cast out with hatred, would narrow its green eyes at her, when she emerged from the house. She paid it no attention, but it agitated her, and she took care that it didn't look for a chance to sneak inside again. She was jealous of everything that came into contact with her little queendom.

When she got up in the morning her first job was to carefully wipe all the places that Teo had touched. She took pains to wipe out signs his presence, if she couldn't wipe him out.

When she saw the snake, stretching its living brown body along the edge, Petra felt a vague threat. A threat to her connection with the house. She screamed, but not from fear, but from frustration, that something else was coveting the only thing she had in this world.

Teo heard her cry and ran up straight away, ready to defend her from the devil himself.

It was then that Petra remembered everything she'd been told about the house. It was as if someone else was lifting her arm and pointing upwards with whitewash covered fingers and was speaking on her behalf: "As long as that thing stays unfinished there'll be God knows what pests turning up," she hissed.

Teo was about to open his mouth, but Petra, turned and decisively slammed the door in his face.

He remained a long time looking after her, then he turned and over the fence he met Mavri's gaze.

On his way to the house of Belinko's second wife, Mavri saw everything, he gave Teo a sympathetic look and hurried away.

He was passing by the gate of Belinko's second wife, ever more frequently and openly, and his eyes were only fixed on her. Wasn't it the case that now there was no man in this house? Only his persistence had forced the other men to stand aside and watch on silently.

Once quite calmly, Mavri pushed open the gate and entered. He crossed the yard, took the axe from the hands of the second wife, detached her from the woodpile and continued to cut the wood with abrupt sharp movements. The axe glinted for a second above his head. He collected the firewood and carried it to the house front door. He left it and turned his smiling face to Belinko's second wife. His teeth gleamed like his shirt and Belinko's second wife smelled the wafting whiteness and strength. Timidly she stretched out her slender hand and gently patted away the wood shavings stuck to his chest.

Mavri bristled as if from the cold, the garden span before his eyes, a quiver passed through his body and sat in his throat. He swallowed hard, took a deep breath and raised his eyes.

And he saw Belinko's face, glued to the window opposite, staring fixedly at them.

When he met his eye, Belinko pulled back and disappeared within the house.

31

Petra carried out Teo's bedclothes into the little room at the end of the corridor, where his Granny, old Krayanka had died. He understood that as long as he didn't get down to fixing the terrace, she wouldn't let him near her. But he didn't blame her, he put it all down to her fear of the snake.

I'll start tomorrow, Teo thought, and the snake won't appear and Petra will take me in again, and everything will be so lovely, as it can only be with her...

He never forgot his Granny's words, that he'd heard from early childhood, that a snake in the house is the soul of the first homeowner. He loved his granddad, in his childhood memories he saw him as a big strong old man, who'd tossed him in his huge strong hands. Granddad would play with him, caress him, care for the little boy, and Teo would always remember him with tears in his eyes. He remembered the first appearance of the snake and how it had passed over his hand like a caress. Then he'd been happy that his Granddad had come to stroke him, often after that he'd climb up to the terrace and look for the snake... But now Teo was angry and if the snake popped up in front of him he would chase it away ot perhaps – he was scared to think of it, he'd kill it... Because of Petra. So she wouldn't be afraid. So she would take him back. So that meant he'd be killing the snake for his own good as well.

It was dusk, he walked round the yard, sunk in his thoughts and he looked at the place where he'd be setting the new balcony. And he wanted to start right away. Only for one short moment the fracture of the supporting beam popped into his memory and the collapse of the balcony, and his Granddad's arms and legs sticking out from under the huge fragments... Teo scratched his head and rid himself of the dark thoughts. He climbed up to the second floor, and looked out from there. His gaze slid over the yard, beyond the house, over the low cottages all the way to the sea. The sea could be seen from the second floor windows. For the first time Teo wondered why Petra hadn't chosen a room for them here. He'd seen for a long time but never questioned why Petra avoided the sea and kept to the earth, as low as possible and closer to her.

Up on the cliff he saw the upright tall figure of the Sailor.

Teo trembled from sudden cold and hurried to get inside.

In the night a storm blew up, one of those early autumn storms which resemble hurricanes. It bent the trees, it bashed the old bell tower and made it ring. Its toll had not been heard in the village for a long time, since the old verger had departed in his turn. And the old took their final journey without the village knowing.

In this horrific night, the bell rang on its own and with its random ringing, mixed in with the howl of the storm, people's hearts were squeezed by horror and bad premonitions.

They knew that this time too, the Sailor had untied his boat and launched into the roaring waves.

In this night Petra went to Teo in the little room. She snuggled up to him in the narrow iron bed, squeezed him close and shaking hid her terrified eyes in his strong body.

Teo encircled her with his strong arms and hugged her. For the first time he felt big and strong. He felt like a man. He felt like a protector. And he confidently towered over her quivering body and covered her frightened face with kisses.

Petra gradually began to calm down under his caresses and surrender to his manly strength.

CHAOS

Beneath the crashing of the raging storm two days and nights fused into one night only.

Only on the third day in the evening did the wind gradually die down, and simply stopped in the night.

The whole night, Teo was listening. He made sure that the storm had passed and barely waited till sunrise, he hugged Petra's body that curled into him. Grey dawn light began to penetrate through the curtains and he got up carefully so as not to wake her, kissed her tenderly and rolled up his sleeves. Petra muttered something in her sleep and smiled as she hugged the pillow.

Teo went out into the clear cold morning and began to work. He first erected a beam like a pillar then climbed to the second floor and put in the support beams. He'd found them in a hut at the bottom of the garden and it never occurred to him that in all the years they'd been left there, the beams might have rotted.

He finished this work early in the afternoon, and he began mixing the concrete. From time to time he cast his eyes towards the windows expecting to meet Petra's gaze.

Petra did not appear, she was showing no interest in his work. Happy that Teo was not getting under her feet inside, she stayed on her own in her bedroom. She closed the curtains completely and shut her eyes, lay beneath the thick eiderdown, pressed her body close to the wall. And as she took in the breath of the house, the previous endlessly long night with Teo on the narrow iron bed passed before her eyes. Her fingers, whitened and stiffened by the plaster sought the deep furrows she'd gouged in the wall.

Outside Teo worked without a break. He didn't stop even to grab a snack. Now that he'd discovered that he could have power over Petra, subdue her, and feel her tender self, so fragile that any moment it could break in his hands, he was scared he'd lose her again. He'd never been a builder, he didn't know how to lay a floor, but hadn't he seen Belinko's work, he was sure that he could manage as well. He carried bucket after bucket up to the first floor, he poured out the concrete over the support beams, they bent under its weight, he'd smooth it out and then go down for another bucket. The kitten followed him as always, from the garden to the first floor and back again, assiduously stalking him, not missing a single step...

And when the beams broke and the balcony cracked and fell down, from under the big shards, Petra dug out along with Teo, a little crushed ball from which two still living eyes looked at her in pain.

Somewhere close by Granny Vanda was passing, but she stepped aside, crossed herself and continued, muttering angrily out of the side of her mouth. Some vague troubling premonition quivered through her, but the old woman paid it no mind, obsessed as she was with her wish to avert the evil that she felt approaching.

Granny Vanda stopped out of breath before the gate of Belinko's second wife, but she did not enter, but shouted curses and orders from outside.

Belinko's second wife was working in the yard and as if she hadn't heard just took the children into the house.

"You leave him be, to look after his family!" Granny Vanda was shouting. "He's got five children! And his wife is honest, not like you..."

Granny Vanda had never interfered with her son's life, but had watched on in silence. She had not shown a clear dislike towards her daughter-in-law. Only now with the threat of a new woman, and Mavri following his father's crazy path, the old woman took her daughter-in-law's side. And she was fighting for her, for her son, for his family. And for herself. The way she should have fought some time back when she was young. She'd tell everything to this nobody, she'd tell her even what she'd left unsaid to that other woman, whom she'd discovered in Elo's hut... Everything, piled up by the man who'd left her, without even waiting for the birth of their son, she was now going to pour out over Belinko's second wife.

CHAOS

Ey, these men, Granny Vanda shook her head, can't they come to their senses?... It wasn't easy for Mavri, with no father and look, now he too was ready to cut off his sons.

One memory suddenly invaded the old woman's inner eye and stopped her talking for a moment. Mavri was seven or eight, when he ran, trembling up to her, grabbed her hand and began pulling her. Worried, Vanda set off after him. The child led her to the next-door yard. Standing in front of the window which served him as a mirror a fisherman was shaving. The sharp razor took the foaming soap from his face and revealed a smooth rosy skin, slightly blue under the shaven chin.

"Mum., what's he doing?" the boy asked frightened and held her tight.

And then Vanda understood how important a man's example was to young boys. She understood that you have to fight tooth and nail for your man, and keep the father of your son at any cost.

Her eyes moistened with the memory. She hadn't kept Elo, but she would protect the father of her grandsons. She'd fight and keep him with his family. She wiped her tears with a quick flourish, lifted her head and took a deep breath to continue. Yesterday when she had talked a long time with Mavri, in a voice quite louder than usual, and explained to him how important it was for him to stay with his sons, he had just said, "She too has sons..." with which he put an end to the conversation and left.

Granny Vanda was not now going to allow any interruption to everything she wanted to say.

Unexpectedly the other woman called out quietly, "What can I do when you've given birth to such a handsome guy..." and she lifted her mild bright eyes to hers.

The old woman froze with mouth wide open. Not so much because of the words, which warmed her maternal heart. Not so much because of the woman's beauty which she was seeing for the first time close up and felt with her heart. But from those bright eyes, which looked so much like Elo's and his three children's, his tormented soul too was looking at her. The chaos which smouldered somewhere deep within Mavri, which Belinko bore too, was also latent within this woman. Some vague suspicion flitted through Granny Vanda, but she quickly rejected it.

No, it's not possible, the old woman thought. Aren't they the same blood as Belinko, and you can't know how their children will be... And their kids are hale and hearty and quite normal... No, it can't be that, there are enough crazy folk in the world.

She sighed out her gathered breath noisily, stood frustrated, turned and set off down the street with diminished steps without saying another word. A shrunken old woman with eyes seeing far into the future but with a spirit of acceptance.

"She's not to blame," Granny Vanda continued to sort things out in her head. "Woman is created to seduce... Especially a beautiful woman... Man is the one who has to keep his wits. But a man's wits are often not where he needs them."

As she passed back by the Krayan house she heard Petra's cry and put a stop to her thinking. She entered the yard and saw Teo's crushed body under the concrete shards. She turned her accusing eyes towards Homeless Petra. And Petra realized that she could not pull the wool over her eyes. She lowered her head, crouched down and began to clean up around Teo. Granny Vanda helped her, both of them lifting his smashed body, dragging him into his little room and dumping him on the tall iron bed.

"Is he sleeping in this room?" Granny Vanda asked in a loud voice and fixed her eyes on the Homeless one.

Petra took a step back.

Granny Vanda carefully covered Teo and again fixed her accusing eyes on her.

"You have to look after him very well!"

CHAOS

Petra nodded and lowered her eyes.

The old woman turned and left. Outside she noticed the kitten, left in the same place, where the slab had caught him.

Up on the edge the snake stretched indifferently.

Granny Vanda saw it, she crossed herself and almost ran away from the Krayan house.

32

No-one paid any attention to the kitten. It was barely able to crawl to a corner of the yard, close to the outside gate and there it curled its smashed body. Sometimes it opened its eyes painfully and looked out in hopes of seeing if Teo would appear.

Only Petra would appear from the house and would pass it by without a glance. It forgot its dislike of her and its quiet whimper grew louder to catch her attention. She pretended not to hear it and she hurried her step. The kitten again let its head flop down with a deep painful sigh.

The same painful sigh was heard from Teo's room when Petra's footsteps passed somewhere down the end of the corridor.

She only appeared once a day. She'd leave a pan with something thrown together, by his head and hurry to leave. She was afraid that he might chance to reach out his hands to catch her and make her sit a while with him. She was scared of meeting his fading eyes and see the pain in them. The door would slam behind her and her steps would echo round the house.

Two great tears would course down Teo's dried yellowing face. He didn't want to believe, he refused to accept everything that Petra was doing. It was chance that she left the food by his head in such a way he could not reach it, she was so careless. She didn't even suspect that he could not move his arms and couldn't shift his broken body at all. The next morning when she picked up the pan, she surely assumed he had eaten, she was so distracted. She'd not forgotten everything they'd lived through together... She'd not forgotten their last night in the storm. Teo believed that. He wanted so much to believe...

Then the suspicion crept inside him. That had never happened, it never was, he'd dreamt it. And now he wanted it to be true, to have happened... Pain befogged his mind, plunged his thoughts in black murk. His arms lay thin and helpless, at his two sides, estranged from his body. Loneliness weighed desperately on the little room and his moaning turned into a long sad sigh that carried throughout the house.

33

Belinko stuck his face to the second floor window and silently observed his second wife's yard. This window turned into his favourite place. It was his little secret. His first wife would go out, and he often sent her out, he'd climb upstairs and stick to the window. He turned himself into a prisoner. He was ashamed of showing his nose out in the village, meeting the sniggering looks of the men. And most of all he was afraid of looking into the eyes of his second wife. Or the eyes of his young children that were filled with bewilderment. He forbade himself to go out and from here he'd follow his two boys as they played around their mothers' skirts. He'd see how Mavri would enter the yard like a proprietor and get down to the man's work. He worked deftly, his muscles would ripple under his white shirt and underline his agile movements. The second wife would watch him from one side, tell him something, her voice reached the window and bounced off it. Mavri would finish everything, he'd grab the older child and begin to toss him up. The boy would shriek for joy, and the yard would ring with their laughter which would jump over the fence, sneak through to him inside and attack his ears.

Mavri had not entered the house yet.

When would this happen, Belinko sighed and the chaos inside him increased and awoke a hitherto dormant fury. Fury towards his second wife, towards his first wife, who had condemned him to this secret imprisonment, towards Mavri, and most of all towards himself. He pressed his face to the glass to cool it down.

CHAOS

In the yard, his second wife was feeding the cats and talking to them lovingly. Mavri was not there and Belinko looked on calmly. His first wife wasn't around either, she'd gone out early in the morning and still hadn't returned. And where did she go, he angrily wondered, then settled the question, they must be at the shore. He felt a strong desire to go, to walk round the rocks, to see folk, talk with the men, go out to sea in the boat. He hadn't seen anyone for so much time, hadn't talked to anyone, he didn't want to talk to his first wife either. He only saw her and hatred slowly piled up.

He knew why the village had rushed to the shore. Several days had passed since the storm had died down, but the Sailor still hadn't come back. Folk were roaming round the rocks looking for him.

34

The fishermen roamed the shore, circled the harbour. But they didn't go out to sea, they were waiting.

"He's drowned," one of them said.

The children didn't believe them. And they didn't believe themselves. Or they didn't want to believe.

"Going out in such a storm..." Others shook their heads, but they looked expectantly out at the horizon.

Mavri's sons stood on the cliff and fixed their eyes on the sea. Some of the fishermen with their wives climbed up beside them. They stopped in front of the house and hesitated. One woman took the decision, cautiously stretched out a hand and clutched the door handle. The door was unlocked, it opened with a drawn out creaking and everyone peered inside. There was no-one there.

The children were frightened, they stepped over the threshold with bated breath.

A thick layer of dust covered everything, it was wiped only in the few places, which seemingly the Sailor had touched. Over a chair, almost white with dust, hung a woman's old, colourless, short coat, looking almost like a person. Mavri's eldest son reached out his hand to carefully touch it. It came apart in his fingers, from its many years and turned into a pile of ash. The lad jumped back in horror and ran outside. The others followed.

They returned to the shore, walking along the water's edge, looking for signs, if only the sea had thrown up something. The boys peered into the shallows, checked the furthest rocks, but found nothing. Only in the hidden creek where they'd seen Homeless Petra for the first time, they found a broken oar.

The people stopped, looked at one another and sent Mavri's second son to call Granny Vanda.

While the old woman was descending from her house to the creek, people looked at the oar, turned it back and forth, passed it from hand to hand and in the end gave it to her.

Granny Vanda took it and looked it over. Everyone waited for what she'd say with bated breath.

"He's gone to his wife," she spoke quietly.

People understood her. They turned this way and that, but soon returned to their homes.

Granny Vanda stayed alone. She took the oar and left, she'd take it to her home, like a document.

"Come on, be off with you too," she turned to the children. "You've got no reason to sit here…"

For the first time, the children didn't believe her.

"He'll come back," they said.

They climbed the cliff, they sat down and dangled their feet over the abyss, without feeling the rain which had begun to drizzle quietly.

The children were waiting. They had a whole life of waiting in front of them.

35

During the day Petra kept away from the corridor so as not to hear Teo's moaning. Now she didn't go to him at all, didn't bring him food, she couldn't look at the grey skin that hung off the protruding bones beneath her. Sometimes something began to stir her conscience and trouble her thoughts, some inner voice expressing doubt, but she quickly rejected it.

In the night she'd slip into her room, she'd lock the door in the face of her worries, to keep them out and she tried to take in only the noises from the house. She'd undress slowly in the dark, nestle into the huge empty bed and press her hot body to the wall. She's stroke it with hands and feet rubbing her flaming skin into its coolness.

On the next day her skin was burning even more, with scratches all over. Petra would touch them with her stiff whitewashed fingers and a sweet pain spilled through her body.

She'd go out into the yard and stand in the rain. The cold drops soaked into her clothes. The grazed places spread with whitewash made her look like a plaster statue. The wet soaked into her like into the parched earth.

The kitten lay beneath the rain without moving. It no longer lifted its head, only from time to time a quiver through its matted fur showed it was still alive. The rain drops couldn't chase away the huge green-black flies which for the last two days had stuck to it and would not let go.

36

Belinko's second wife sent her children to play in the barn in the dry along with the cats and stayed smiling at the gate, unaware of the rain.

As always Belinko was watching from the window opposite. An unpleasant premonition suddenly stabbed him and he stood fully alert. His eyes darted from his second wife to the street and back, taking in every movement, her every quiver.

In a little while, Mavri appeared in the street, dressed in his whitest shirt. The raindrops soaked into it and glued it to his body, emphasising his muscles. He stopped in front of the second wife and caressed her with his eyes. Without a word they both plunged into the house.

The chaos rose within Belinko, squeezed his throat, choked him. His face changed colour, his mouth was open and he tried painfully to take in at least a little air. Gradually he came to himself, he was panting, he felt his legs, his arms, moved them and tore himself away from the window. He ran down the stairs, shoved past his first wife who was standing inquisitively in his way, and crossed the yard with a couple of strides. He jumped over the fence, looked around and saw the axe which glinting meekly by the woodpile. He grabbed it and rushed towards the house.

His second wife met him at the door, in a long white shirt, with her blond hair spread out over it.

Belinko stopped in confusion. "Where is he?" he roared and he tried to move her.

"He's not here!" she did not let him pass.

In helpless fury, Belinko grabbed her arm and dragged her to the woodpile. He pressed her hand over the wet wood and brandished the axe overhead.

The second wife did not tremble.

The first wife peered through the open door of the house opposite. And she like Belinko had been watching through a window, but on the ground floor, and she'd seen Mavri's arrival. Simultaneously happy and scared, she stepped back and pushed home the bolt. She didn't want to have anything to do with this.

"I'll kill you!" Belinko's voice was grating in helpless anger. "I'll cut off your hands, I'll cut your entire body into pieces and I'll kill myself..." His voice trembled with treacherous tears.

The axe finely cut the skin of her fingers, leaving red furrows in them. The rain washed them into a pink foam. Belinko's second wife clenched her teeth, tightened down her throat, so as not to make a sound and prayed for Mavri not to appear. She'd sent him to the attic and told him not to come out whatever happened. She stifled the pain and looked Belinko right in the eye. Under her gaze he softened like wax, he shrank, his hand gradually let the axe slip, but this turned him angry again. The rain-washed features of his face tightened, the moist eyes narrowed in fury at his own weakness. The second wife knew that in a moment he would be crying and pouring out in the tears, his fury, his desperation, his pain from his sin, his plea to her ... But then she realized that something would happen, that something had already happened. Belinko's turned his eyes away from hers, his features suddenly hardened. He straightened and swung somewhere behind her back, and the axe flashed a second above Mavri's head...

37

The next day the rain stopped.

Petra came out of the house, looked around and saw the kitten's emaciated little body close to the door. She cautiously prodded it with her foot and unmoved she established that it was now stiff. A plump fly was crawling on its protruding tongue and was trying to penetrate its half opened teeth to get into its mouth.

And only the next day the flies appeared in Teo's room.

38

Granny Vanda stayed at home, in spite of the rain having stopped. She sat on her chair by the window, her knitting hung loose from her hands. With her dry eyes she saw through to the deep hole of pain which had unexpectedly opened up.

She must surely have taken a wrong step somewhere, the old woman thought. I should have been watching all three of them. They needed me, needed my help. Only I knew their father's crazed soul. Elo went away, but he left his destructive force in his three children. Mavri, and Belinko and Petra all had it, it destroyed everything around them, destroyed them as well.

Granny Vanda pressed her pale forehead to the glass, listened to herself and realized that she could not turn back time.

39

When she came back from the graveyard, Petra pulled up her sleeves and set to cleaning the house. Till late on, she washed, polished and chased away the big green-black flies which buzzed through every room. By the time she finished the sun was setting.

She bathed slowly and caressed her whitewashed body with her stiff frozen fingers. She took out her festive clothes, the ones Teo bought her for their wedding. She put them on slowly and ceremonially and set out for her room.

That night Homeless Petra would be married to the house.

She opened the door quietly and entered the room with fear and respect. The curtains were closed and the room was sunk in dark.

Petra froze, struck dumb and timid in her excitement, she inhaled the scent of the house, drank it in, held on to it. She took in every noise and it echoed within her. Quivering she approached the bed.

With every step something unfamiliar was controlling her. It imparted not security, but fear, and the closer she got the more the feeling of horror overwhelmed her. She could not bear it, she turned to the window and with a sudden flourish drew back the curtains. Only then did she see.

On the big bed cover the snake was stretched out with all its length. Its head was raised and its split tongue aimed an angry hiss at Petra.

The soul of the house did not accept her. The house's first owner would not give way to her.

And Petra ran.

40

In her escape in the dark, Homeless Petra did not see the unknown men who took Belinko away.

She did not see that following them almost immediately, the "sister" of Belinko's first wife turned up – he'd clearly been hiding up till now – a huge red faced brute of a man. He loaded up the property from the two identical houses and took her away too.

No-one knew where the second wife had disappeared along with the two children. The cats disappeared with her too. That night huge well fed rats crawled out through the yards.

Homeless Petra didn't see the rats either.

Standing on the cliff, she'd absorbed the ink of the night. The dark swallowed her into her chaos. The dark surrounded her on all sides, she saw nothing. Everything was only night. Somewhere very high up and far away a solitary star twinkled. A bird's croaking broke out from the forest then suddenly stopped. At this it was as if the dark grew even heavier and blacker. You could not tell where the earth finished and the sky began. Even the sea was hidden.

Standing over the abyss, with nothing supporting her from below, suspended alone in endless black space, Homeless Petra heard all of eternity cry out with her: "Who will love me now?"

And she turned and descended, lonely, very lonely, with shoulders hunched under the weight of her isolation. She set out through the village, more inland, ever more inland and further away.

41

Granny Vanda kept a small sack of wheat. Just in case, Mavri and his wife had none for the moment she was dispatched on her final journey. And now she had to prepare the same wheat for Mavri's final journey.

The old woman opened the cupboard with a sigh. She stretched out her hand for the sack, but quickly pulled it back. Two huge rats were eating up the last grains.

She shut the cupboard doors and went outside. Her eyes fixed on the walnut tree.

She remembered that today Mavri had to thrash it. They'd collect the walnuts and he'd divide them. One walnut to the left, ten walnuts to the right...

A hot wave rose up and moistened her eyes, in the end two tears ran down her wrinkled cheeks. She lifted her hand and the sleeve of her recently knitted cardigan drank in her grief. She picked up a stick and began thrashing the tree as far as she could reach.

The tree had grown large, long ago the trunk had exceeded the width of her neck and Mavri's. Then she'd found peace. She would depart first, and Mavri would see her off... In many years' time he'd depart too, seen off by his sons, who then would be grown men, and by their sons... And everything would be as it should, since the world came to be. And look how it messed up.

Granny Vanda brandished the stick. She was no longer thrashing the branches, but beating the tree. It's horrible when we see our children depart before us, a voice was screaming inside her. And she laid it on.

Later she got tired and she calmed down. Didn't they have the same father, how wouldn't blood come through in the pair of them?

She bent down and began to gather walnut after walnut from the ground. As there was no wheat, at least she could give folk walnuts... just so they pray for God's forgiveness... There hadn't she planted the walnut because of Mavri. So he'd be strong and healthy and wait for his father...

And so still slowly she began to break them, walnut by walnut, gather the kernels in a tray and when it was full she stood up and set out for the village...

42

The village was horribly deserted.

The houses gaped empty.

Granny Vanda peered into one, then another... Everything was in its place – furniture, coverings – even the left over salt fish hanging under the eaves. Only the doors were open and there were no people.

Carrying the tray with walnuts, the old woman darted between the houses, her steps echoed on the cobbles.

Somewhere ahead she saw a lorry, as tall as the house it had stopped in front of. With breathless steps, Granny Vanda made for it.

"We're leaving, Granny Vanda," the man who emerged grinned at her.

He left the door open and made for the cab.

"What? Why?" the old woman could barely speak.

"We're going to something new... In the town. We've got a whole district for us, and we'll work in a factory," he spoke hurriedly.

"But the village?" with her dry throat she could barely get the question out.

"They'll make a resort here," the fisherman was already getting on board, his wife was making impatient gestures from inside. He stopped and answered in a changed tone with an exaggerated worried giggle, "The sea hasn't got any fish anymore. We can't feed our children... And we can't feed ourselves. Then don't you see what's happening here?"

Granny Vanda lowered her eyes, then she peered through the window and saw the untouched furnishings. "What? Why?" she asked again, because she didn't know what to say. "Are you not taking anything?"

The man just shook his head. "Didn't I tell you, everything new..."

"But your mother gave birth to you on that bed," she pointed inside with her feeble hand.

There was a quiver of rebuke in her voice.

"The wife doesn't want it," he lowered his voice and closed the cab door.

The lorry started up.

Granny Vanda was left perplexed. She lowered her head and saw the tray of walnuts in her hand.

"Take them... so God forgives Mavri," only now did she remember to hold them out.

The lorry revved and disappeared behind a cloud of dust and smoke.

The old woman looked after it a long time. She turned and set off for her house, along the deserted streets. Her hand clawed the walnuts from the tray and scattered them on the ground.

"Walnuts for Mavri... Walnuts for Belinko... And for Petra... for the three of them, Elo's children, beautiful, messed up, restless like him. Walnuts for the Sailor and his wife... For the Krayans and all their family...For Belinko's mother and Peter the Tree's wife, the mother of Petra. And for Elo who left all of them... For Granddad Nacho with his new black suit and for his Granny Visha, with the linen lace sheet... for the old verger..."

Granny Vanda presented everyone with a cast walnut, as she wandered the village's deserted streets. She listed everyone and the tray emptied. The old woman went back to her house...

43

The sun sank.

Sitting under the walnut tree Granny Vanda had taken off the black cardigan and was slowly unravelling it. And look, Mavri was born, began to walk, now a teenager, left home... and now his first son was born, the second, the third... the fifth. The ball of wool was bobbling in her hands and growing with every untied stitch. And life is like that, thought the old woman suddenly, one is born over the ruin of another...

The old woman wound the last stitches into the big black ball and let her tired hands fall with it into her lap. The low sun lingered on her pale whitened dry eyeballs.

"I have to be going now," she whispered.

She did not say this to herself. She did not say this to anyone else, there was nobody around. She said it to her long-past life which still did not want to release her. Everyone had departed from her one by one. First Elo left, even the child who she was expecting did not stop him. He didn't look for him to see him, he didn't look for his other children. Men like the children of women they love. And Elo didn't love any woman. He didn't love anyone. She wasn't sure if he loved himself either...

She got up stiffly, took the chair and went inside. She came out again with the ball of wool in her hand and stood at the end of the yard over the sea. She turned and looked back over the deserted village. Only now she remembered that it was autumn already, and she had to sit inside the house till the end of the winter.

LYUDMILA ANDROVSKA

The leaves of the trees fell one by one and their black naked branches reached out towards the sky like dried up praying hands. The abandoned houses were silent deserted. The bell was silent above them.

Granny Vanda turned and fixed her eyes on the Sailor's house. In the falling dark, she seemed to see a shadow on the cliff-top. A silhouette of a young woman, wrapped for winter in an old coat. No, Granny Vanda stared, it wasn't a woman; that was the tall figure of the Sailor, looking out into the sea.

So there would be a storm, the old woman thought, and felt how a feeling of serenity took her over.

From the sea came a breeze and it blew towards the village.

Her hand let the black ball go and it rolled down towards the water. The thread unravelled and marked its path towards the sea.

Granny Vanda's eyes followed it till it disappeared, then they looked up at the sky.

It was getting dark fast. The wind strengthened, waves appeared.

I have to go now, the old woman thought and looked towards the rising darkened water. Everyone left. Only I remained. Take me, sea... Look how old I am, I lived my life a long time ago. I outlived my child. I want to depart from here, where people rejected the life that our ancestors lived... Where they helped the love depart that we have always waited for... And they rejected you too, sea, which always fed us and deserted the land which bore us...

Behind her the wind raged, tore off roofs, lifted them, smashed them over the forest. It returned, blew harder and began to gather up the walls of houses. A strong gust smashed the bell tower and a drawn out clang echoed over the village.

It grew dark ever faster. The waves became larger and began to pull at the black thread of the ball. Yet another clang was unleashed above them, sad and lonely.

CHAOS

Someone appeared and set out after the black thread. Was it the man who had once left her and taken away her youth with him? No, this was her son... Mavil in his long white shirt.

The sea was pulling and swallowing the thread, and they followed it. They were leaving her, again deserting her... And she wanted to leave...

And Granny Vanda set off after them.

About the Author

Lyudmila Androvska is a Bulgarian author, publisher and screenplay writer.